Room

Preston's Mill, Book One

NOELLE ADAMS
SAMANTHA CHASE

This book is a work of fiction. Names, characters, places, and incidents are the product of the author's imagination or are used fictitiously. Any resemblance to actual events, locales, or persons, living or dead, is coincidental.

ONE

Heather Carver was finally moving back home.

She'd been born and raised in Preston, a small town in eastern Virginia, but she'd been living in Charlottesville for seven years as she went to college and graduate school. She'd always intended to return to her hometown and join her father in business, and now that she'd finally earned her MBA and packed up her little apartment near campus, she was ready to come home.

This weekend she was staying with her father, but on Monday she'd head back to Charlottesville, collect her little Yorkie named Lucy from the friend who was watching her, load up a U-Haul, and drive back to a gorgeous two-bedroom unit in Preston's Mill, an old cotton mill her father had converted into apartments.

Everything was going according to her plans, and she couldn't have been happier or more excited as she pulled a chicken-and-rice casserole out of her father's temperamental old oven.

He owned Carver's Restoration and Construction—a very successful company that specialized in high-end and historical restoration work—but he couldn't be bothered to replace the appliances in his own kitchen.

"It's done," she called out to her father, who was watching the news in the living room. "No oven catastrophes tonight." One never knew whether the oven would decide to complete a dish in half the time or not at all.

"Great. Get me a beer, will you?"

Heather smiled and shook her head as she dished up casserole for her father and carried it out with another beer. Whenever she visited, she ended up waiting on her dad, but she didn't really mind. He'd worked really hard in his life, and he'd basically had to raise her on his own since her mother had walked out on both of them when Heather had been eight.

Her mother had never been around to take care of them, so Heather was happy to bring her father dinner in his recliner.

After she'd returned to get herself some food, she noticed her father looking at her out of the corner of his eyes. "What?" she asked.

"This is great." He nodded toward his plate. He'd been a handsome man most of his life, and he was still in good shape, with salt-and-pepper hair and the same blue eyes that she had.

"Good. But it looked like you wanted to say something else."

"I'm about ready to retire." He said the words like he was announcing he wanted to play golf that weekend.

Heather almost choked on her bite. "What? Already? I thought you were going to wait until you were at least sixty-five. You're just turning sixty this year."

"I know. But I'm tired, and I want to have the freedom to do the things I want to do. Play more golf. Maybe travel some."

Since she'd finally processed what he was saying, she was able to smile at him encouragingly. "Of course. I totally understand. I'm ready now to take over. You know how I've been looking forward to whipping all your accounts and processes into shape."

Her father had carried the business on the strength of his construction and carpentry skills and his personality. His paperwork had always been very sloppy, and Heather had been helping out with the business aspects of the company since she was in high school.

When he just took another bite of casserole, she added, "You should definitely retire and take it easy now, if that's what you want."

"Yeah, but I'm worried." He wasn't looking at her. His eyes were focused on the newscaster on the television.

She'd been about to take a swallow of beer, but now she stiffened her shoulders, feeling a flicker of worry for the first time. "What are you worried about? I'm really good at this stuff. I was near the top of my class in the MBA. You know that."

"I know. But you can't do the hands-on stuff."

He'd taught her some basics when she was a girl, but she'd never been particularly interested in working with tools. Even as a little girl, when her parents had made birdhouses together and tried to get her interested in their hobby, she'd been more inclined to organize the birdhouses into rows by size than actually build them.

She tried to fight a wave of automatic defensiveness since it felt like her dad was telling her she wasn't good enough to run his business when this was what she'd been planning for and looking forward to most of her life. "I know. But you've got crews to do all the construction work. I'd just supervise and take care of the business end."

"But you need someone who knows his stuff to head up the work."

"I could hire someone to do that if none of your guys are ready yet." She did her best to control her voice, so she didn't sound too emotional. But ever since her mother walked out on them, her father was the one person she could completely trust to never leave her, to be completely loyal, and now it felt like he was abandoning her because she wasn't good enough.

It had been her dad who had fixed her school lunches and gone to her ballet recitals. It had been her dad who'd volunteered to help with her field trips and who'd cheered the loudest at her high school and college graduations.

She'd always assumed she'd be the first person her dad would turn to when he was ready to retire.

She'd been hungry before, but she couldn't bring herself to take another bite.

"I've got someone in mind who'd be perfect." Her father still sounded relaxed, laid-back, as if none of this was a big deal.

She took and released a quick breath, feeling better again. Of course her dad wouldn't try to push her out. What had she been thinking? "Oh, that's good. I'd be happy to hire anyone you think best."

"I wasn't thinking of hiring him. I think he needs to be a partner."

"What?"

"It'll only work if he has an equal share in the business."

"You're not going to leave things with... with me?"

"Sure I am. Of course I am. I just think you need a partner."

It hurt—that he didn't trust her enough to take care of the company he'd built. But she'd always prided herself on being a good-natured, reasonable person, and she made herself think through the situation before she reacted emotionally.

He had a point. She might think she could hire someone to supervise the actual construction work, but her father would probably feel better if there was someone who had a genuine vested interest in seeing the business succeed. He wasn't betraying her. He'd never do that. He just wanted to protect the company he'd worked so hard to build.

"Okay," she said. "Whatever you think best is fine with me. It's your company, after all, so it's obviously your decision. Who did you have in mind?"

As soon as she asked the question, she knew—she *knew*—who he had in mind.

Her attempt at being reasonable flew out the window as she saw her father slanting her another look.

"No," she choked, putting her plate on the coffee table so she wouldn't accidentally dump her food on the floor. "Not Chris! Please tell me it's not him."

"Of course it's him. Who else?"

"But he abandoned you! After all the years you spent teaching and training him, he just walked out on you."

"He had his reasons."

Like Heather, Christopher Dole had been raised in Preston, and he'd started working for her father in high school. He'd taken to the work quickly, and her father had soon become his mentor, teaching him everything he knew. Chris was three years older than Heather, but she'd gotten to know him really well—since he was always hanging around the house and the company offices. She might have had a little crush on him on and off through her teenage years, although he'd never acted at all romantically toward her.

He'd been an important part of her life though—hers and her father's. Until three years ago when he'd walked out on them to take a high-risk, high-paying construction job in Alaska.

Heather was naturally easygoing and personable. She wasn't in the habit of holding grudges or getting into arguments. Most of the people she knew she liked—even the annoying ones. But Chris was the one person in her life she couldn't forgive. He'd hurt her father. He'd betrayed all her dad's trust and emotional investment.

He didn't get to waltz back into their lives now and grab up half her father's company.

"Well, his reasons aren't good enough," she said, not able to keep her voice as level as she had before. "I know he was upset when his mom died, but that doesn't mean you give up everything and everyone. That doesn't mean you betray someone who was like a father to you."

"He didn't betray me."

"Yes, he did. He *did*."

"It's time to let all that go. We've been talking, and he's decided to come back home and help me out."

"Why didn't you tell me you've been talking to him?"

"Cause I knew you'd be mad and upset about it. I didn't want to bring it up until I had it all worked out."

"So it's a done deal then? You're going to give him your business?" She was trying very hard not to cry. She didn't want to be one of those children who expected all their parents' success to fall their way just because they were related, but it was hard not to feel hurt by her father's decision.

They'd always talked about her taking over the company when her dad retired. She'd been planning on it for so long, loving the idea of preserving part of her father that way.

"Not the whole thing. I want you and him to be partners. It's the best way to keep the business a success."

She swallowed hard. "Okay. I know it's your decision. I'll try to get along with him—for you."

When her father slanted her another quick look, she knew he wasn't finished with his revelations. "Yeah, see, that's the thing."

"What's the thing?"

"It's never going to work unless I know you two are able to work together."

"I'll do the best I can."

"I know you will, but I need more assurance than that. So I came up with this idea."

"What idea?"

"Since I need some concrete proof that you and Chris can get along enough to run the business when I'm gone, I figured you two could live together for six months in that apartment in Preston's Mill. If you can make it that long in close quarters, then you'll do fine with the business."

She'd lifted her beer to take another swallow, but now she froze with it halfway to her mouth. Her eyes widened about double their normal size. "*What?*"

"You heard me. Chris needs a place to stay anyway, and the unit has two bedrooms. After six months, he can move out, and I can pass on the company to the two of you, knowing you're not going to destroy it because you two can't get along." Her father's eyes were still on the news, and ridiculously he looked almost amused, as if this were some sort of game.

It *wasn't* a game. "You've got to be crazy!"

He arched his eyebrows at her.

"I'm sorry, Dad. I don't mean to be rude, but seriously, this is just… crazy. I can't live with Chris!"

"Then you won't be able to work with him."

"Working is different than living with him. I promise I can get along with him. We don't have to go through a ridiculous stunt like this to prove it."

"I'm not so sure. You're usually the nicest person in the world. Everyone in town adores you. And yet you've always had this animosity toward Chris. I want to make sure that goes away."

She took a few deep breaths and tried to rein in her outrage. "You're serious about this?"

"Dead serious."

"So if I want to take over your company when you retire, I need to…"

"Live with Chris for six months."

"And this isn't some little joke you're playing on me?"

"No joke. I've already run it by him, and he's willing."

"I don't believe that. He was just as mad at me as I was with him when he left."

"That was three years ago. I'm sure he's gotten over it."

"Like I have?"

Her father seemed to hide a laugh. "Okay. Maybe not. But you both are reasonable people. I'm sure you'll learn to get along in such close quarters. You can do something else if you'd rather—move somewhere else, get another job. I don't want you to, but you're free to do that if you'd rather. Otherwise, Chris is moving in. He said he'd be in town on Tuesday or Wednesday."

She stared at her father for a minute, trying to read his expression. Finally she concluded he was absolutely serious.

It was his company. He could do whatever he wanted with it. And he could put any sort of conditions he chose on the people he wanted to leave the company with.

She didn't have a choice.

If she wanted to be a partner in her father's business—which she'd been planning on since she was ten years old—then she'd have to live with Christopher Dole for six months.

For six months. In one fairly small two-bedroom apartment. With one bathroom. And one big, handsome, obnoxious, disloyal man.

This wasn't at all what she'd expected for her return to Preston.

She made it through the rest of the evening with her father, mostly by trying to forget what he'd told her, but she left the house with a heavy clench in her gut.

She wished Lucy was with her. Her dog was the most faithful of companions. She never dropped bombshells like her father just had, leaving the foundations of her world rattled.

As she walked down the sidewalk, she paused when a glint of light hit a delicate birdhouse hanging in one of the trees that lined the yard.

She remembered the day her mom and dad had made that birdhouse. She'd been seven, and they hadn't shut themselves into their bedroom to argue all day—which meant it was a very good day for Heather. Her parents making those birdhouses on the weekends had been the best times she could remember. They'd been happy. She'd felt safe. The world had functioned the way it was supposed to for those few hours.

She'd always wondered why her father had kept all the birdhouses he'd made with his wife, even after she'd abandoned them.

Heather brushed the memories away as she got into her car. Her throat was tight, but she wasn't going to cry.

Her father had always been there for her, and he'd never wanted anything but the best for her. So if he was so adamant about this ridiculous roommate scheme, then she was going to do it.

~

On Monday, just before noon, Heather pulled the small moving truck up to the entrance at Preston's Mill.

She'd made it in from Charlottesville an hour early, and the guys her father had gotten to help her move her furniture wouldn't show up until one. That was fine with her though. She could scope things out, bring in some smaller items, and decide where to put all her stuff.

She'd decided to leave Lucy with a friend until tomorrow so her dog wouldn't be so upset by the moving commotion. But she was planning to be fully settled—with Lucy joining her and all her possessions unpacked and where she wanted them—before Chris arrived tomorrow or Wednesday

Over the past few days, she'd come to terms with her situation. It was a ridiculous plan. She didn't think her father was getting senile, so he must just be indulging a whim.

Maybe he was feeling nostalgic for the old days, when Chris had felt like part of their family. Maybe he was trying to reconstruct their old relationships by forcing the two of them together now.

Whatever the reason, she loved her dad more than she hated Chris.

After all, she and Chris would have their own rooms. She was willing to spend most of her time in her bedroom if she had to. They could basically ignore each other at home.

The main thing was to avoid getting into fights—if they were going to prove to her father that they could get along.

She could do this. It was only six months, after all.

She walked up the stairs to the second floor, carrying her purse and an overnight bag. Her unit was at the end of the hall on the corner. As she walked past the adjacent apartment, the door opened without warning.

Heather jerked in surprise and stopped to see an elderly lady poke her head out into the hall. The woman's hair was full of those pink sponge curlers she thought no one used anymore. "Oh," Heather said with her normal friendly smile. "Hello. I'm your new neighbor, Heather Carver."

"Estelle Berry. I know your father," the woman said, narrowing her eyes as she looked Heather up and down.

"Oh, do you? It's very nice to meet you, Mrs. Berry."

"You seem like a very polite young lady, so you can call me Estelle. So is this some sort of modern arrangement then?"

Heather blinked. "I'm sorry?"

"You and that hunk of a mountain man in there." Estelle nodded toward the door to Heather's unit. "Do you and him have one of those modern arrangements, where sexual relations are had without a wedding ring?"

Heather was so confused and startled that she looked between the old lady and her front door. "No," she managed to say. "No. There are no sexual relations being had." Ridiculously, she felt her cheeks flushing.

"Good. I'm glad to hear it." Estelle pulled her head back into her own apartment and closed the door in Heather's face.

Heather stood there for a full minute, trying to figure out what was going on. She finally realized something that she should have put together much earlier.

There was a "hunk of a mountain man" in her apartment.

Chris wasn't supposed to arrive today.

She walked slowly down the rest of the hall toward her unit. When she tried the door, it was open.

Her father had done a great job with this building. All the apartments were lovely, and this one most of all. The ceilings were tall, and the beautiful dark hardwood floors were original. One wall was exposed brick, and another was full of tall windows. The sleek modern kitchen opened to the main room, separated by the dark granite of the island.

Heather loved this place, but she felt a sinking of her stomach when she saw a pile of boxes and an ugly orange recliner stuck in the middle of the living area.

What the hell was Chris doing here already?

She was staring at his recliner—right where she'd been planning to put her pretty red slipper chair—when he emerged from one of the bedrooms.

Chris had always been good-looking with his broad shoulders, easy smile, dark eyes, and cleft chin. When she'd known him before, he'd always kept his hair short and been clean-shaven.

He wasn't anymore.

He looked like he'd just slunk out of a cave. His beard was long, his hair untrimmed, and both his jeans and T-shirt were torn. He was bigger than she remembered, and he seemed to take up all the space in the big room.

She'd intended to act friendly toward him, but she was too flustered to say anything but, "I thought you weren't coming until tomorrow."

"I got here today." His voice was low, gruff. He was staring at her with those same dark eyes she remembered, and he wasn't smiling.

"I can see that." She took a deep breath, tearing her eyes away from the breadth of his shoulders and the size of his biceps. He'd been strong before, but it looked like he'd been tearing up trees by the roots for the past few years.

They'd been screaming at each other the last time she'd seen him. She'd been berating him for abandoning her father, and he'd been saying over and over that she had no idea what was going on with him.

It was the worst fight she'd ever had, and it suddenly felt like it had just happened yesterday.

She'd trusted him before, and it had been one of the worst mistakes of her life.

Her gaze landed on the door he'd emerged from. That was the room she'd been planning to claim—the one with the best view and larger closet. Her mind whirled with confusion and annoyance and resentment and something like anxiety, but she tried to sound her typical upbeat self as she asked, "So you're taking that room?"

"Yeah."

If he'd been a gentleman, he would have offered it to her, but she knew better than to believe he was anything like a gentleman.

It didn't matter. She wasn't going to get into an argument on their first day here. She just had to make it through six months. She could keep a smile plastered on her face for that long, and then she could mostly be free of him.

"Did you want it?" Chris added, when she didn't say anything.

She shook her head with a fake smile. "Of course not. The other one is just fine."

She walked into the bedroom and dropped her stuff on the floor, giving herself a mental pep talk about keeping her composure.

It was just Chris. He wasn't—and he'd never been—that important to her. She could paste on a smile and pretend he didn't exist for the next six months.

Right?

When she felt up to it, she peeked out into the main room and was relieved when she didn't see him. She stepped out and noticed that his bedroom door was closed.

Good. Maybe he had the same thing in mind that she did. Stay out of each other's way as much as possible.

There was only one bathroom in the apartment, but it was a big one with a freestanding soaker tub, a lovely tiled walk-in shower, and a granite-topped vanity. She went to use the bathroom and then stared at herself in the mirror as she washed her hands.

She looked like her normal self—smallish with long blond hair, her eyes and mouth a little too big. She'd pulled her hair into two braids to keep it out of the way as she moved her boxes, but she suddenly wished she'd done something prettier with it.

Not that she wanted to attract Chris. Not at all. She'd sooner hook up with old Jack Turner who lived downstairs and only showered once a month. But still. She didn't want Chris to look down on her in any way, and right now she looked like a little girl.

She blew out a breath and resisted the urge to take her hair out of the braids. She wasn't going to primp for him. She wasn't going to change anything about herself for him.

She was turning to leave the bathroom when the door started to open.

She couldn't hold back a squeal of surprise and indignation. "Hey! I'm in here." She swung the door opened all the way to glare at Chris, who was standing there looking rather stunned.

"I thought you were back in your room."

"I'm not back in my room. I'm in here. When the bathroom door is closed, then you either knock or you wait."

"Okay. Fine." His brows were lowered as he studied her. "I heard the toilet flush a long time ago. What were you doing in here?"

For no good reason, she was embarrassed that he'd heard her flush the toilet. And she certainly wasn't going to admit that she'd been standing there, trying to steel herself to face him again. "That's none of your business. Just knock on the door next time."

"Fine. I will." He didn't look happy to be here. He didn't look like he liked her. But he also didn't look angry at her.

And that bothered her a little bit too. That he could upset her so much after just a few minutes and she couldn't upset him at all.

She reminded herself it didn't matter. She was going to pretend he didn't exist to the best of her ability, and she wasn't going to let him see that he could upset her like this again.

TWO

Chris shut off his alarm and let out a long, weary sigh. What the hell had he been thinking to agree to this arrangement? Yesterday had been awkward enough, but luckily there had been the distraction of Heather moving her stuff in to keep them from actually having to talk too much.

Except to argue.

Damn, but the woman certainly knew how to do that.

About everything!

With a muttered curse, he climbed from the bed and stretched. It was only five thirty in the morning. He had purposely set the alarm for this early so he could have a little time to mentally prepare for their first official day of... well, everything. Roommates. Business partners. What the hell was Tom thinking of with this crazy arrangement?

An overwhelming sense of guilt washed over him for a minute. It usually did when he thought of his friend and mentor, Tom Carver. The man had been the one source of stability in his life for so many years, and how had Chris thanked him? By running off as soon as life got a little tough.

So maybe this was payback.

The thought made him laugh. It would be fitting too—forcing Chris to not only work with the man's daughter, but live with her too. He shook his head because, although he realized what the lesson was they were supposed to be learning, it just still didn't sit right with him. The entire thing.

Heather was always a good kid—quiet, studious, and easygoing. That was not the woman who had walked in yesterday like she owned the place.

Well... technically she did. Sort of. But the quiet girl he remembered was gone, and in her place was a woman who wasn't afraid to speak her mind.

About everything.

With shuffled steps, Chris walked out of his bedroom and into the bathroom. The apartment was dark and peaceful, and after quickly relieving himself, he stepped out into the kitchen to make some coffee. As the liquid brewed, he looked at the mess in front of him. There were boxes everywhere, and it was a hodgepodge of furniture.

He chuckled as he remembered Heather's instant dislike of his orange recliner. She'd been glaring at it as he'd come out of his room yesterday to see her for the first time. Once his coffee was made, he walked over and ran his hand lovingly over the piece of furniture. Flo. That's what he'd named her. The orange fabric reminded him of a character, Flo the waitress, on a television show his mother had always watched, and so he'd been calling the recliner that since he'd gotten it. She was the most comfortable piece of furniture he had ever owned—other than his king-size bed—and although she wasn't the prettiest piece of furniture ever made, he loved her.

"Do you two need a moment alone?"

Chris froze at the sound of Heather's voice. Why was she up so early, and more importantly, why hadn't he thought to put on pants? Looking down at his boxers, he immediately realized that he was going to have to make some adjustments to living with Heather.

Namely? Wear pants.

Dammit.

17

Forcing a smile on his face, he looked over at Heather. "We're fine with expressing our love in front of other people." She didn't smile at the joke. Clearing his throat, he took a sip of his coffee and motioned over toward the kitchen counter. "Coffee's ready. Help yourself."

If he wasn't mistaken, she made a face before turning and walking toward the kitchen. He studied her as she moved and mentally noted all the ways she'd changed in the three years he'd been gone.

The girl he remembered didn't have the same grace. She didn't move with the kind of ease that Heather was moving with now. And she certainly didn't walk around in short little robes that showed a lot of tanned, toned legs.

Swallowing hard, he quickly turned away, but it was too late. Certain parts of his anatomy were way ahead of him in noticing her skimpy attire, and now...

"Oh my God!" she cried from across the room, and Chris jumped into the recliner before she could see his response to how gorgeous she was. "What on earth is this?"

He had to stifle a laugh when he realized she was referring to the coffee. Yeah. He liked it really strong. Like... really, really strong. Most people hated his coffee, and judging by the carrying on going on behind him, it was fairly safe to say that Heather did too.

Chris heard her slam the mug down while muttering about bad coffee and how she should have just made her own and his overall lack of manners because he lived like a mountain man and...

Wait... *what?*

Standing up, he walked back to the kitchen. "Mountain man? What the hell does that even mean?"

Big blue eyes looked back at him, like a deer caught in the headlights. It was really hard not to laugh this time

18

because it was obvious that she not only thought he had no manners, but that he couldn't hear either.

"Oh... um... I just meant that you..."

He leaned casually against the granite countertop and sipped his coffee, amused by her sputtering since she normally seemed so composed.

"You could have warned me that the coffee was that strong, Christopher."

Christopher? Hell, the last person to call him Christopher was his fourth grade teacher, Mrs. Kelly. And his mom.

"Obviously you've been living in some sort of wilderness, based on the looks of you," she was going on. "And maybe you've forgotten basic common courtesies, but—"

"I'll have you know that no one on my last job complained about my coffee," he said as he took another long drink.

"Really? Were they ever forced to drink it?"

She had him there, but he wasn't ready to admit it. "No one forced you to drink it either. You did that at your own risk."

"My own..." With a huff, Heather walked past him toward a stack of boxes in the corner of the kitchen and began moving them around. Five minutes later, she was back with some sort of... hell, he didn't know what it was, but she was putting it on the counter next to his coffee maker. "This," she said breathlessly, "is what modern, non-mountain people use to make coffee now."

He frowned. "What have you got against mountain people?"

"What... I don't have anything against them."

He arched a dark brow at her. "Are you sure? Because you keep throwing that phrase around like you've got a serious grudge." Then he stood back, finished his coffee, and watched as she tried to come up with a snappy comeback.

And realized this was kind of fun.

Normally, he preferred the peace and quiet of a morning alone—it was a great way to get his head in the game for whatever work was in store for him that day. But bantering with Heather had him more engaged than he could remember being in... a really long time.

Stepping past her, he poured himself a second cup of coffee and grinned at her as he walked back over to Flo to sit down.

"Can we talk about moving the furniture around for a minute?" she said from across the room.

"Sure. What were you thinking?"

"Wait... give me a minute."

One of the many good things about Flo was that she also spun around. So he turned and watched as Heather put some sort of pod into the machine she just put on the counter. It made a humming noise, and then she had coffee. Interesting. He was so focused on the coffee maker that he didn't notice those tanned, bare legs coming his way. Quickly spinning Flo back around, he took a sip of his coffee.

Heather took a seat on the sofa that was facing him. "I would really like to get this place put together a bit today," she began. "I think the couch works here, and the coffee table is spaced nicely. But maybe your recliner would look better... in your room." She looked at him sweetly as she took a sip of her own coffee in some sort of flowery mug.

"You want me to put Flo in my bedroom?"

She straightened and looked at him oddly. "Flo?"

He rubbed the arm of the recliner.

"You seriously named that chair Flo?"

"Yup. And she stays in the living room. Where else am I going to sit while I watch TV?" He studied Heather for a moment and saw a world of frustration play across her face. "Any other suggestions?"

Now it was her turn to arch a brow. "I'm sure I can think of one."

"Sarcasm… nice," he said with a grin and then stood and stretched. "Flo stays, but I'll make you a deal. You can move the rest of this furniture around any way that you like, as long as she stays right here."

"But it's so ugly!"

He ran a hand lovingly over the top of the recliner and leaned down toward it. "Don't listen to her, baby. She'll come around."

"Christopher," Heather called out as he turned to walk away.

He stopped and looked back at her. "Look, I'm not any happier about this setup than you are," he began, realizing suddenly that this was going to be life for the next several months. "It's six months. If you don't like the chair, tough. I'm sure by the time you get your things unpacked I'm going to find something of yours that I don't like too. We'll just have to deal with it. Okay?"

He didn't wait for an answer. He stormed off to the bathroom to take a shower.

Twenty minutes later, he looked at his reflection.

Mountain man.

Yeah, it had been a while since he'd shaved. Or gotten a haircut. Or given a damn. He was looking pretty rough. At the back of his mind, he'd always assumed he'd clean himself up some after he got back to Preston, but if he shaved right now, it would look like he was caving to her and her mockery. Then again, he was supposed to be getting ready to take over Tom's business, and it wouldn't be right to look so… unkempt and unprofessional.

So he made a mental note to hit the barber later today and let someone else help him start to look human again.

The bathroom wasn't overly large, but Heather's stuff was everywhere—makeup, jars of mysterious creams, and just general clutter. They were going to have to figure out a better system for this. And fast. Drying off, he wrapped a towel around his waist, brushed his teeth, scooped up his stuff, and opened the door.

Heather turned and looked at him, her eyes going a little wide before she turned away. Okay, so a towel wasn't much more than the damn boxers. Note to self: pants! Seriously. Take pants with you everywhere.

~

It was close to six that evening when Chris was standing at the door to their apartment with a mixture of apprehension and exhaustion. It had been a long day. He'd spent a large part of it getting reacquainted with the town and driving by some of the job sites Tom had told him about. Then he'd gone to get that shave and a haircut. He ran a hand along his now-smooth jaw and had to admit it felt pretty damn glorious. He'd forgotten how freeing it felt to be clean-shaven. So clearly beards weren't for him. Good to know.

He felt a little bad about not helping Heather with her unpacking, but he had a feeling she probably preferred it that way. He'd had the advantage of arriving first, and he didn't have much with him to unpack. Plus he was a guy, and he didn't overthink the placement of every item he owned. He had a feeling Heather did.

No doubt he was going to find that everything was put in a specific place, and if he tried to move it, he would get his head bitten off. He chuckled. "Bring it," he murmured.

But he still didn't open the door.

But someone did. Down the hall.

"Young man! What are you doing loitering out here in the hall?"

He turned around and saw an elderly woman standing in the doorway to the apartment down the hall. She was tiny and had a bunch of pink rollers in her hair—the kind his grandmother used to wear. And she was scowling at him.

"Um... excuse me?"

"You heard me," she snapped. "What's the matter? Did you forget your key? Or did that pretty girl throw you out?"

"Um... I... I was just..."

"Of course in my day, we didn't throw handsome men out of the house."

Oh my God... was she flirting with him?

"It's a good thing you shaved. Show her you're sorry and that you're making an attempt to look nice for her."

"Who exactly are we talking about?" Chris took a couple of steps toward her. "And I don't think we've been properly introduced... I'm Chris. Chris Dole."

"Christopher is a nice strong name," she gushed, and for a minute, he swore she was blushing. "And I'm Estelle. It's lovely to meet you." She held her hand out for him to... kiss.

Fabulous.

So he did and then had to admit he kind of liked the small giggle she let out before taking her hand back. "So... Estelle. Who am I trying to look nice for?"

"Heather," she replied firmly. "Although now that you're all cleaned up, maybe I'll have to talk to her again about your modern arrangement."

He had no idea what she was talking about and was starting to get a headache. "Modern..."

"Heather said there was no hanky-panky going on between the two of you, no sexual relations, you understand. But you sure did clean up nicely."

Now he was blushing!

"You should go," Estelle said. "Wheel of Fortune's about to start, and I don't want to miss it." Her door slammed shut, and Chris could only stand in stunned silence for a minute as he tried to comprehend what had just happened.

Shaking his head, he walked to his door, let himself in, and just as he'd suspected, the place was completely decorated. There were throw pillows on the sofa and pictures hung on the wall. But luckily, Flo was exactly where he'd left her.

He shut the door and was about to call out to Heather, but she walked into the room and came to a halt at the sight of him. No doubt she was noticing that there was a whole lot less hair on his head and face. He braced himself for the mountain man comment.

"Good. I'm glad you're back. I've written up some ground rules for us to go over," she said as she went to sit down at the kitchen table.

Rules? No comment about his hair?

Rather than argue, he went and sat down beside her and chuckled when she slid a sheet of paper in his direction. "You printed out the rules for us to live by?" he asked incredulously.

"It seemed the most efficient thing to do. I just drafted up some to begin with, and we can discuss them."

He rolled his eyes and then settled in to scan the page. But he was completely aware of Heather sitting there watching him—as if waiting for him to find fault with something.

And he did.

"I'm not agreeing to number three."

She instantly picked up her copy and scanned it. "And why not?"

"Because I enjoy watching TV late at night. I'm not going to let you give me a curfew. That's crazy!"

"It's not a curfew. But I like to go to sleep at a reasonable hour. You can't tell me that you have to have the television on full blast late at night."

"Ah, but it doesn't say that here, does it? All it says is no TV after eleven. What am I, ten years old? We're roommates, Heather. You're not my mom."

She sighed loudly and crossed it off the list, and he went back to reading. "And number seven is stupid."

"Why?" she asked, clearly irritated.

"I'm not splitting the refrigerator in half. Believe me, I'll know what food is yours and what's mine. I don't think we're going to have that problem. And if by some chance I eat some of your peanut butter, I'll go out and get you more."

Chris read the rest of the list and then stood up and grabbed both copies and crumpled them up.

"Hey!" Heather objected, coming to her feet. "What in the world? We're never going to be able to work this crazy situation out if we don't have a few ground rules."

He spun around and stood facing her. "Here's the deal—we both live here, and neither one of us should be dictating how the other lives. You want rules, here they are. You buy your own food, I'll buy mine. You cook for yourself, and I'll cook for me. Neither of us should be expected to wait on the other one. You with me so far?"

She nodded, although her eyes were narrowed as if she weren't thinking happy thoughts about him.

"Good. You clean up after yourself, and I'll clean up after me. Okay?"

She nodded again.

"We're both going to pay equal parts on the utilities—fifty-fifty. I take quick showers, and I put my dishes in the dishwasher, and I turn out lights when I leave the room. If you insist on taking hour-long showers and washing every piece of silverware by hand, I'm gonna amend that rule and ask you to pay more on the water bill."

"Same applies," she countered. "If you end up using more of the utilities."

"Fine by me." Then he paused. "We're not joined at the hip. We may have to work together and live together, but we have separate lives. If we want to ride to work together and save on gas, great. But it's not a requirement."

"Agreed."

And as much as he tried to think, they seemed to have covered all the basics. "If either of us comes up with something else, we'll talk about it. No lists. No dictating, deal?"

"Deal."

"Do we, uh… do we need to shake on it?"

Heather seemed to consider her options and held out a hand to him. "Sure. Why not?"

Taking her hand in his, Chris immediately realized his mistake. Her hand was small and soft, and he got a little jolt of awareness at the contact. He quickly pulled his hand away and took a step back.

"So, um, it looks like you got a lot done here today. It looks good."

She beamed at his praise. "Thanks. And you'll notice that your chair is exactly where you left it."

"I did and thank you." Okay, maybe this wasn't going to be so bad. They were capable of having decent conversations without animosity, it seemed. Maybe clearing the air was the way to go.

"It's certainly an eclectic look—more so than I'm used to, but I think it will work. And like you said earlier, it's only for six months."

She smiled at him—a genuine smile—and Chris felt himself relax. There was a time when they'd been friends, and although the last time they'd been together—three years ago—they'd been screaming at one another, this was the girl he remembered.

Only… prettier.

Softer.

With great legs.

Down boy. He needed to get comfortable in the friend zone here. They had six months of living and working in close proximity to one another, and he could not afford to let himself think about her as anything but a business partner and roommate. This was too important. He refused to let Tom down.

Again.

Clearing his throat, he walked over to the refrigerator and opened it. "I only grabbed a few things from the grocery store yesterday, so I think I'm going to order a pizza for dinner. I was driving around today and saw that Tony's was still there."

She nodded. "Still the best pizza in town too. Maybe we could split a pizza?"

Her voice and her expression were hopeful, and Chris readily agreed. "Pepperoni?"

"Like there's anything else," she said with a laugh, and Chris definitely felt more relaxed. He called in the order and made arrangements for it to be delivered. "How long?" she asked.

"Thirty minutes. I think I'm just gonna go and…" A small jingling sound had him stopping in his tracks and looking around.

"Is something wrong?" Heather asked, and he noted a small smirk on her face.

"Did you hear that?"

"Hear what?"

Waiting, he held up a hand when the jingling sound happened again. "That! I heard a jingling sound. What do you think it was? It's not a sound you'd hear from the plumbing, and these walls are fairly thick and well insulated, so we shouldn't be hearing anything from the neighbors."

The jingling got louder, and when he saw exactly where it was coming from, he was mildly horrified. "What… what the… Where the hell did that come from?"

Heather's smile grew as she bent down and scooped the tiny… well, it looked like a dog, but it could have been some sort of rodent too. She walked over with… it… in her arms. "This is Little Miss Lucy," she cooed.

"Uh, what?"

She rolled her eyes and snuggled the *thing* closer. "Little Miss Lucy. She's my dog."

"Are you sure she's a dog? Because she looks like a rat."

"No, she doesn't! And that's just mean." She stroked the dog's back and kissed her on the head. "Don't pay any attention to him, my little miss."

He studied the dog and had to fight the urge to cringe. It was tiny—maybe five pounds—and it had pink bows in its hair and some sort of sparkly collar on. It looked completely ridiculous. "So… Lucy," he said.

Heather met his gaze. "Little Miss Lucy."

"Yeah, I'm not calling her that."

"But it's her name."

He raked a hand through his hair as he sighed with frustration. "I might call her Lucy but honestly, I'll probably just call her dog."

The look of horror on her face told him that it was the wrong thing to say.

"Look," he quickly added. "I'm not a dog person, and I'm really not a tiny dog person. Can't she just stay in your room?"

And then that look of horror turned to a look that was maybe just a little bit evil. Heather stepped in closer as that evil smile grew. "Oh no," she began. "She can't stay in my bedroom. She likes having room to roam around, and besides, I like to cuddle with her while I sit and watch TV."

Then she put the dog down. "I'll just go and grab some cash for my share of the pizza."

And in that moment, he knew the battle lines had officially been drawn.

THREE

The next day, Heather came home after work feeling encouraged. Almost optimistic. Maybe this ridiculous arrangement wouldn't be as bad as she'd feared.

Today had gone better than yesterday. Other than looking at each other over coffee mugs in the morning, she'd barely seen Chris all day. He was annoying—no doubt about that. And way too smug. And he didn't even seem to be sorry for the way he'd treated her father three years ago. But he appeared to agree with her that they should mostly just keep to themselves. If they were able to continue doing that, then they'd make it through these six months without too much trouble.

Hopefully.

As she was leaving the office this morning, her father had mentioned that Chris was supervising the crew at a job they were running behind on, so they'd be working until at least seven this evening. That gave her two hours in the apartment alone.

Another reason to be in a good mood.

Deciding to take advantage of the privacy, she dropped her purse on the floor in the entry hall, crouched down to greet an ecstatic Lucy, and then walked into the bathroom, turning on the water in the tub.

She'd been looking forward to making use of the soaker tub. Now was the perfect time.

While the tub filled, she took Lucy outside and made a quick batch of cookies. She'd made a batch yesterday and had given them to Estelle Berry, and today she wanted to make a batch for old Mr. Johnson downstairs.

She'd learned when she was a girl that making cookies was such a simple thing to do, but it made people so happy, made them feel appreciated. She'd been giving friends and neighbors cookies for most of her life.

It just took a few minutes to mix up the dough, and while they were in the oven, she poured herself a glass of Merlot, turned on some music, and lit a few candles in the bathroom. After she'd taken the cookies out of the oven to cool, she pulled off her clothes and got in to soak, leaving the door partly cracked so Lucy could come in and out as she liked.

Otherwise, the dog would scratch at the door insistently. It was just barely five thirty. Chris wouldn't be home for an hour and a half.

The tub was amazing—long enough to fit her body and deep enough for a very enjoyable soak. She relaxed, letting her mind drift and occasionally chatting to Lucy when the dog wandered in to investigate the situation.

After about twenty minutes, Heather opened her eyes when she heard the sound of a door close.

It was probably just Mrs. Berry or another one of the neighbors. The walls were thicker than a lot of newer builds, but one could still hear a lot of noises from the hallway. She leaned back against the tub and closed her eyes again, wondering what had Lucy all excited.

Her little claws on the hardwood floor were tapping like crazy.

"Heather?" The male voice was familiar, but it was also shocking since it was coming from the doorway to the bathroom.

The doorway to the bathroom!

Her eyes shot open, and she squealed when she saw Chris looking in, Lucy dancing ecstatically at his feet.

"What are you doing?" she gasped, trying to hide under the water until she realized that there were no bubbles to hide beneath. She'd only put in some lavender-and-honey-scented bath salts. "What are you doing here?"

Chris blinked, his gaze focused decidedly lower than it should be. "I live here."

"But you're not supposed to be here until after seven!" Her mind shifting quickly into crisis mode, she grabbed her towel, which she'd fortunately placed within arm's reach, and lifted it to cover herself as she stood up.

"Was that a rule I missed?" His voice was dry and gruff, as usual, but he was decidedly distracted, his eyes raking over her bare, dripping legs and the damp towel.

She scowled at him and gestured to her face. "Eyes up here."

He managed to raise his eyes to meet hers. "You're the one taking a bath with the door open."

"That was for Lucy!" She was flustered and embarrassed and also just a little bit excited, although that last reaction was probably just a fluke.

"She likes to leer at you while you're naked?"

"No! She likes to come in and out. You weren't supposed to be home until after seven."

"Why do you keep saying that?" He seemed amused now, although his eyes did occasionally drift back down to her body. "I didn't realize you'd given me a schedule."

"Dad said that you were working at the Harmon job until after seven." She managed to say this more lucidly since she realized squealing wasn't the best way to express her quite reasonable assumption.

"The crew is working. But there was no reason for me to stay there the whole time."

Typical of him to slack off before the job was done. He was always walking away when things got hard. She decided not to say so though since she was genuinely trying to get along with the man. "I didn't know that."

"I can see that." He frowned as he glanced around at the flickering candles. "Why do you have all these candles lit and the music on? I thought you might have someone here with you."

Naturally his mind would go immediately to her getting it on with some guy in their apartment. She gave him a prim little frown. "There's no one here with me. I thought, since you weren't here, I'd have a little private time."

"Oh." Something changed on his face. "*Oh.*" The second time, he drawled out the word, stretching it out far longer than it should have been.

It took her a moment to realize what he was implying. When she did, she gasped and hugged the towel to her more closely. "Not like *that!*"

Did he actually think she was in here with the candles and music, having a little fun with herself?

"Ah. Too bad. That would have been something to walk in on."

He was teasing her, she realized. Making fun of her responses. With effort, she reined in her indignation. "Now if you don't mind, I'd like to put some clothes on."

"No problem." He started to leave but glanced at her over his shoulder, his dark eyes deliciously warm. "Next time you want a little private time, maybe hang a sock on the door."

She almost—almost—laughed.

Then he added, "Who are those cookies for?"

"They're for Mr. Johnson. Don't eat any!"

"Not even one?"

"I didn't make them for you!"

She normally wouldn't have been stingy with cookies, but she was too rattled now to be generous. And mostly she wanted him out of the bathroom.

He was grumbling as he closed the door.

He really was much too good-looking, now that he'd gotten rid of all that extraneous hair. He looked more like he used to look, when she'd considered him part of her family, when she'd thought he was the best guy in the world.

She sighed as she pulled on her robe and blew out the candles.

He wasn't that guy anymore.

~

Heather spent most of the evening in her room since it was the only place that really felt like hers. She actually ended up falling asleep early, and she woke up at eleven at night, realizing that Lucy would need to go out once more before bed.

She was wearing a tank top and a pair of pink cotton pajama pants, and she decided she was dressed more than adequately to be seen by Chris. After all, if they were roommates, she could hardly be worrying about covering every inch of skin anytime she left her bedroom.

When she stepped out of her room, the first thing she noticed was her traitorous little dog, curled up right in Chris's lap.

The second thing she noticed was there were two men in the living room, when she'd expected to only see one.

She jerked to a stop, staring at the second man, who was sitting on her pretty red chair. He was cute in an absent-minded way, with thick, rumpled hair and a half-turned-up collar.

"You remember Jace Foster?" Chris asked. "He was in my class at school. I just discovered he lives downstairs."

Heather frowned, trying to place him. Jace was good-looking, although not as good-looking as Chris, and he looked both easygoing and intelligent. "Sure," she said slowly. "It's good to see you."

"She doesn't remember you," Chris said with a wry smile.

"You probably remember me with glasses," Jace said, not looking remotely offended. "I was on the chess team."

"Oh, yeah!" She smiled, pleased that she could now place the man in her memory. "You used to always hang out with Isabella Warren."

"Evidently, he still does," Chris put in.

Since this sounded rather snide, Heather ignored it. She came closer, still smiling at Jace. "You look great. I never would have recognized you."

"Thanks," Jace said.

At the same time, Chris muttered, "He doesn't look *that* great."

This comment made Jace laugh and Heather frown. She didn't know why the man always had to be so rude.

She was about to say something else friendly—to Jace, not to Chris—when she noticed that the eyes of both the men weren't exactly staying up on her face. She glanced down at herself and was startled to see that her nipples were tight and poking out visibly through the thin fabric of her tank top.

Okay. That was a little too much for mixed company. She was relieved to see the belted sweater she'd worn to work this morning flung across a stool at the granite bar. She stepped over to grab it, covering up the objects of their distraction.

"I need to take Lucy out before bed," she said, snapping her fingers. "Lucy."

The dog lifted her head from Chris's lap and gave her a look of quiet indignation.

"Lucy, come!" Heather snapped with more authority. She wasn't going to have her dog switching loyalties to someone like Chris.

This time the dog heaved herself up and jumped down from the ugly orange recliner.

The recliner named Flo.

"I better be getting home," Jace said, getting up and leaning over to pet Lucy. "It was good to see both of you. I'll see you around." He smiled at her. "I'll walk you down."

Heather smiled back, studiously ignoring the fact that Chris was glowering.

She called for Lucy once more, and they walked out to the hallway. As they were passing Estelle Berry's door, it flew opened.

The woman must spend half the day looking out her peephole.

"Isn't one young man enough for you?" she demanded, still wearing those same pink sponge rollers. Heather had never seen her without them.

"What?"

Estelle gave Jace a disapproving look.

37

"Oh, he's not mine either," Heather said quickly. "He was just visiting. He lives downstairs."

"I should hope so. I understand modern arrangements, but a *threesome* would be going too far."

Heather and Jace exchanged amused glances as Estelle slammed her door shut.

They walked downstairs, trying not to laugh. Then she waved goodbye to Jace before she stepped outside. It was still warm out—too warm for the sweater. But she really didn't want to show the world her nipples.

Lucy was usually good about doing her business quickly, since she preferred to be inside than outside. But today she ran around in circles.

Heather watched her, starting to get worried when the circles continued. The dog only did that when she had an upset stomach.

Sure enough, when Lucy finally started going, it wasn't a pleasant sight.

"Oh no! You poor thing. Did you eat something you shouldn't have?" Heather tried to think back to what Lucy had eaten today, but she hadn't gotten anything but her dog food and the few treats she was allowed.

Unless Chris had stuffed the dog full of junk food.

Lucy took a long time getting everything out, and she kept trying even after there was nothing left.

"Are you okay now?" Heather asked the little dog, when Lucy came over and stared up at her pitifully. "Are you ready to go in?"

Lucy wagged her tail just slightly. Then she turned around and started running circles again.

Heather sighed. The poor little thing.

"What's wrong with her?" a voice came from behind her.

She jerked slightly before she realized that it was just Chris. He was still dressed in the jeans and T-shirt he'd been wearing all day, and he was looking at Lucy with curiosity rather than sympathy.

"I thought you got lost out here or something," he added.

"She has digestive issues," Heather said. "She has a very sensitive system."

"Somehow that doesn't surprise me."

"There's no reason to be mean about it. She's a sweet little girl, and she's sick." Heather slanted him a quick look. "You didn't feed her people food or anything, did you?"

He arched his eyebrows. "I didn't feed her anything, but she stole a piece of my bacon this morning."

"No wonder she's sick! How did she steal it?"

"She jumped right up onto a chair and then onto the table, and she snatched it off my plate." He sounded like he still resented the thievery.

"Well, you need to be careful not to leave chairs positioned so she can jump onto the table. She gets sick when she eats people food."

"I can see that." He gave her a quick look. "Don't give me that look. It's not my fault she's a little thief. She can blame her own greediness for her suffering now."

Despite herself, she wanted to smile at his dry, clever tone.

They stood together in the dark as Lucy made her circles on the grass. After a few minutes, Chris asked, "How long have you had her?"

"Four years." Heather sighed. "It feels like I've had her forever."

"She seems quite attached to you."

"She is. And I just love her. It's so nice to have someone who is always loyal, who is always so happy to see you."

"That shouldn't be so unusual for you."

Heather turned her head to look at his face. "What do you mean?"

"I just mean everyone seems to like you. You're always making cookies—for everyone who isn't me. Isn't everyone happy to see you when you show up?"

She kind of liked that he thought that about her. "I don't know. I don't really think so. Not so it feels as completely genuine as Lucy is."

"I don't believe that. You have family and tons of friends. You're not going to convince me that your dog is all you have going for you."

"I didn't mean it like that. I have my dad, of course. He's never once let me down. But he's pretty much the only family I have."

"Your mom is still alive, isn't she?" His voice was different now—softer, almost gentle. Like he was really interested.

"Yeah. She is. But she got remarried when I was ten. You knew that, didn't you?"

"Sure, but that doesn't mean you can't still be close to her."

"I guess. But I'm not. It was like she had a whole new life and I couldn't really be part of it. She calls occasionally, and I might see her once a year, but it's really just... a gesture.

She wanted to move on. When she left my dad, she left me too."

It was a pain that had never fully gone away, and Heather's voice cracked slightly on the last words. She gave Chris a quick look, but he was watching her quietly, no mockery or judgment on his face. "At least she's still alive," she added. "I've got nothing to complain about."

"Maybe," he murmured, his eyes never leaving her face. "But at least I know my mom never left me. She always chose *me*."

Heather swallowed hard, swept with a wave of emotion and deep understanding. It was like Chris had reached in and touched inside her, connecting them in a way she'd never experienced before. She swayed forward, caught up in the softness of his brown eyes and the way he looked in the shifting shadows of the night.

Chris seemed to lean toward her too, but then an unexpected noise jarred them apart.

The sound came from below them, and it was long and stretched and high-pitched.

"What was that?" Chris asked, staring down in the direction of the sound.

Lucy wagged her tail at him.

Trying not to laugh, Heather reached down and picked up her dog. "She had a little gas. Don't laugh at her."

Despite her admonishment, Chris burst into a warm, low laughter. "I thought you couldn't hear dogs do that. Just smell it."

Heather couldn't help but chuckle too as she carried Lucy back inside. "Well, Little Miss Lucy has always been exceptional."

They returned to their apartment and soon went their own ways to their bedrooms.

Heather was relieved that the strangely intense moment between them had been interrupted.

She couldn't let herself fall for Chris despite the way he occasionally drew her toward him.

She needed a man who would commit, and she knew from hard experience that man would never be Chris.

~

The next morning, as she was walking into the office, someone called out a greeting to her from down the block.

She paused as a man approached. She recognized him almost immediately. He was Randy, whom she'd dated briefly in high school. He'd always been kind of wild in his teenage years. He'd ridden a motorcycle and not followed many rules. So Heather was surprised to see him look so well dressed and respectable now.

They chatted for a few minutes, catching up on what the other was doing. He was still living in town, and he worked in his family's restaurant across the street.

When he asked her if she was busy on Saturday night, Heather told him she'd love to have dinner with him.

She wasn't super excited about him, but she liked him and there was no reason not to go out with him.

It would be good to take her mind off Chris anyway.

As if her thoughts had conjured him, she saw Chris striding from his car into the office, looking big and handsome and bad-tempered.

She didn't know why he would be so bad-tempered, but he didn't greet her or even nod as he passed.

She didn't care. She had a date with Randy on Saturday, and she was going to go back to ignoring Chris for the duration of their roommate arrangement.

Things would be a lot safer that way.

FOUR

Contrary to popular belief—and by that he meant Heather's opinion—Chris was a hard worker who took his job and responsibilities seriously. And that meant putting his social life aside while trying to get this business with Tom to a place where everyone was comfortable. Just because the business was solid didn't mean that he and Heather were going to be able to slide into their positions without any effort.

At least, that was the way he viewed it.

Clearly, Heather did not.

Eating a bowl of popcorn, Chris was doing his best to focus on the running chatter on ESPN and not on the fact that Heather was fluttering around getting ready for a date.

A date!

Seriously, what the hell?

She'd been relatively aloof for days, and although he couldn't really speak for her, he knew he'd been busy supervising one job site while stopping in and observing three others. His days had been long and challenging, while sitting in an air-conditioned office clearly left one time to make dates with guys who practically trip over themselves to get your attention.

Damn Randy.

The blow dryer was on, and he could hear Heather humming. With a growl, he picked up the remote and made the TV louder. He was just about to throw the remote when he looked down and saw Lucy staring up at him. Her tail was wagging, and he could almost swear her expression was sympathetic—like she knew he was annoyed about Heather going out while he was stuck at home with no one to hang out with.

Great, now I'm the dog whisperer. With a huff, he put the bowl of popcorn down on the coffee table along with the remote. Just as he as getting situated again, Lucy jumped into his lap—all five pounds of her.

"Hey," he grumbled and was ready to toss her down, but she looked up at him and then licked his hand. The last thing Chris needed right now was this stupid little dog. She was ridiculous to look at. Unable to help himself, he picked her up and sort of weighed her in his hand... yup. She was ridiculous to feel too. Carefully, he put her back on the floor. "Go away."

For a minute, he was afraid that she was going to stay there and stare, but Heather turned off the blow dryer, and the dog seemed to practically skip away to go see her mistress. He snorted with disgust. "Whatever."

Glancing over his shoulder—and the good thing about Flo was how she was big enough to hide behind—he watched as Heather moved from the bathroom to her bedroom. She was dressed in some sort of floral dress. Her hair was curled, and she looked much nicer than she did on a work day. That wasn't saying that she didn't look nice during the week, but she was definitely putting in some serious effort here for the date.

Chris looked down at himself and frowned. It was six o'clock on a Saturday night, and he was in a pair of sweats and a T-shirt—a stained T-shirt at that—and seriously considering eating peanut butter right out of the jar for dinner because he was too worn out to cook. Or order takeout. Not a good sign. Especially considering that his roommate was all dolled up and dressed to kill.

Okay, stop obsessing on that, he admonished himself. With a sound that was suspiciously like an eighty-year-old man, he rose from his beloved chair and went to his room to change. Not that he was going to go anywhere, but so that he might be motivated to eat something that required more of an effort than twisting off the lid and dipping a spoon in.

Yikes.

Five minutes later, he had changed into jeans and a clean T-shirt and walked back into the living room.

"Hey, um, would you mind feeding Lucy tonight?" Heather asked. She was moving her things from one purse to another and didn't really look up at him.

"Yeah. Sure."

"And she'll need to go out a time or two. You know… after she eats. If you don't mind."

He was aware of the dog's schedule. He knew that Heather fed Lucy around seven each night, then took her out at eight and then again before they went to bed. So…

"Wait… how long are you planning on being out?" he asked and almost cringed at how much he sounded like an overprotective parent.

Heather looked up at him in surprise. "Excuse me?'

"I'm just saying, if you expect me to babysit the damn dog—"

"I'm not asking you to babysit," she said with a bit of exasperation. "She eats like a quarter of a cup of food, and you have to just walk down the stairs and watch her for five minutes while she does her business. That hardly constitutes babysitting."

Chris shrugged. "Time out of my night."

She gave him an ironic look. "Seriously?"

"Did you even think for a minute that I might have plans?" he asked, and before she could answer he went on. "What would you do with little miss fur ball if I wasn't here to look out for her?"

Heather sighed loudly. "You know what? Never mind. I'll feed her now, and I'll take her for a walk, and then I'll put her in my room so you won't have to deal with her."

Stepping back, Chris watched as she made her way to the kitchen while muttering under her breath about how childish he was and how ridiculous this entire situation was. Well... he completely agreed. On all of it.

Not that he was going to admit it out loud.

With a shrug, he walked across the room and scooped up his keys. He didn't think it would be possible for him to keep playing nice right now, and he certainly didn't want to be here when Randy showed up to pick her up. So he'd go and grab some takeout and drive around and just... not be here.

Without a word to her, he turned and left.

~

In the back of his mind, Chris seriously hoped he'd run into someone he knew, and then he'd have plans for the night too. Not a date, but just not sitting home alone.

No such luck. Within thirty minutes, he was parked back in front of the building and feeling more and more annoyed about it. Grabbing his bag of Chinese food, he stalked from his truck and was walking up the front path when he stopped in his tracks. Heather and Randy were coming out the door, and he cursed. If only he had taken five more minutes.

They were engrossed in conversation and turned to the right, so they hadn't even seen him. And he wasn't sure if he was relieved or pissed.

With another curse, he opted to be pissed and quickly went inside.

He was almost to his door when he heard a noise he was coming to dread, almost as much as every other aspect of his current life—Estelle's door opening.

"Young man," she said, sounding a little more normal than usual. "Can you help me?"

Well, damn. There was no way he was going to say no to her. Plastering a smile on his face, he turned toward her. "Sure, Estelle. What can I do for you?"

She looked down both sides of the hallway before speaking. "You need to come closer. It's... it's private."

Oh dear Lord.

He stepped closer and prayed he was going to come out of this unscathed. Looking at Estelle, he noticed she didn't have her pink curlers in her hair. For the first time, he could see that it was a light gray and styled. "Are you okay?" he asked.

"I'm having a gentleman friend come over for dinner, and I need to move some things around, but I can't. They're too heavy. Can you help me?"

"You... you have a..."

"A date?" she finished for him and then gave him a girlish smile. "I do. But he'll be here any minute, and I wanted to move the sofa a bit and my kitchen table. Can you help me?"

"Why are you moving furniture for a date?" he asked, totally confused.

Estelle gave him an indignant look. "I don't believe that's any of your concern. Maybe things are easier if some of the furniture is closer together, or maybe I need a little room to spread out. Really, Christopher, it's none of your business. Are you going to help me or not?"

There was no way he was going to start to imagine why Estelle and her date needed to spread out, and he figured the sooner he got this done, the better. Stepping into her apartment, he placed his bag of takeout on her kitchen counter and then moved over to the sofa. "Where am I moving this to?"

Estelle sniffed at the bag of food. "Chinese food?"

He nodded. "My dinner."

"Oh, how nice! I do love some chicken chow mien." Then she paused. "That's an awful lot of food for one person."

He let out a heavy sigh. "Estelle? The sofa? Where do you want it?"

"I saw Heather leaving earlier with a nice young man. They made a very handsome couple. I heard them laughing all the way down the hall." She smiled and then directed him on where she wanted the sofa. "Do you have a date tonight? Is that why you have so much food in the bag?"

"There's really not that much in there."

"Oh. Well, that's too bad."

Chris paused and looked at her curiously. "What is?"

"That you don't have a date," she said, her expression bordered on pitiful.

"I never said—"

"You didn't have to, dear. And here I am blathering on about my wonderful social life and Heather's lucky young man, and you're, well, you're all alone," she added sadly. Then she walked over and patted his hand. "I'm so sorry. It's rude of me to flaunt my good fortune while you're spending the night by yourself."

Good fortune? It was on the tip of his tongue to try to correct her—to tell her exactly why it was that he was alone tonight, but he decided against it. Instead, he hung his head a little and sighed again. "It's all right, Estelle. I'll be okay. Now where can I place that table so that you and your gentleman friend will be comfortable?"

Her smile brightened up, and she instructed him on the placement of the furniture and then thanked him profusely. Chris picked up his bag of food and made a quick beeline for the door.

"Thank you again, Christopher!"

"My pleasure, Estelle. You have a good night." He quickly stepped out into the hallway and gave her a small wave before he turned.

"You too! And if you get too lonely, you can come back and—" She stopped. "Never mind. Have a good night!"

And then she slammed her door.

Great. Even the elderly didn't want to hang out with him.

Well, fine. No big deal. He opened the door to the apartment, walked in, and tried to enjoy the peace and quiet. Kicking off his shoes, he shut the door and walked to the kitchen—stopping to pick up the TV remote and turning on ESPN to see if he could catch a game on somewhere.

Within minutes he was all set—his plate loaded with food and a cold beer. Even though there wasn't a game on that interested him, Chris had found a home renovation show that had captured his attention. He was just about to sit on Flo when he heard a noise. Well, not a noise, but a whimper. A whine. A scratch.

Ignoring it, he sat down and turned up the volume on the television. The forkful of food was halfway to his mouth when the whining grew louder and more insistent. "Can it, Lucy!" he called over his shoulder and quickly ate that first bite of his dinner.

More whining.

More scratching.

The damn dog's scratching was so frantic that Chris was certain Lucy was going to get right through the door. With a muttered curse, he put his plate down and went to Heather's door and yanked it open. The dog pranced out excitedly and began dancing around his legs. He would have thought that with all that carrying on she must have to go out, but she didn't run to the door. She eventually just sat at his feet and stared up at him as her tail wagged.

"So what was all the fuss about?" he snapped. "I was eating my dinner and trying to watch some TV, but you were making such a racket that I had to stop!"

If anything, her tail wagged even more, and she seemed to be smiling at him.

Shit. Dogs don't smile, and he had to be losing his mind if that was what he was seeing.

With a huff, he stepped over her, went back to Flo, and picked up his dinner. The home improvement show host was talking about the way to properly sand down and restore hardwood floors. It wasn't exactly rocket science. It took only a minute before he was arguing with the screen.

"You can't start with a medium-grit sandpaper! You need the course grit to remove all the damn layers of crap! What is wrong with you?"

Beside him, Lucy let out a little bark.

Chris looked down at her. "Right? This guy doesn't know what he's talking about! If you don't start off with a course grit, you'll be sanding twice as long and never get all the old finish off. And on top of that, you'll probably burn out the motor on the sander." He snorted with disgust. "Seriously, how do these guys get their own shows?"

Another bark.

He finished his dinner and took a long pull of his beer. As he was sitting back in his seat, Lucy looked like she was ready to jump into his lap. Without much thought, he reached for her and put her in the seat beside him. "No point in hurting yourself."

They sat like that, watching the rest of the show— every once in a while, Chris would comment on what they were doing wrong and why he'd do it differently. She was in his lap and listening intently to every word he said.

And he kind of liked it.

After the renovation show, another one started up— this time talking about working with stone houses. He loved this kind of thing, and even though Lucy had curled up in his lap and wasn't listening nearly as much as she had a few minutes ago, Chris kept an open dialogue going the entire time—as he petted her.

By the end of a third episode, he was feeling the need to get up and move around. Maybe some dessert. "Cookies would be great right about now, if Heather was ever generous enough to make some for me. Not that she ever will. She'll probably stuff damn Randy full of them though."

Lucy jumped off his lap and followed him to the kitchen. "Oh no. Don't even think about it. You can't handle the big people stuff," he said as he grabbed a pack of Oreos from the cabinet. The damn dog was right there with him— all jingly and happy and tail wagging. He sighed. Looking around, he went to where he knew Heather kept the dog treats and grabbed two of them. "And if you rat me out for this, I'll deny it," he said to the dog as they walked back over to Flo.

So Chris ate his Oreos and Lucy had her treats, and as the dog settled in beside him again, he couldn't help but feel annoyed. Not at the dog. She wasn't so bad. But at the entire situation. Here he was, watching renovation shows and looking at different ways to do things on their job sites, while Heather was out on a date. Why did she have enough free time on her hands to make plans to go out and socialize, anyway?

They were supposed to be proving something to her father—that they could work together and be ready to take over his business in six months so he could retire. Well, from where Chris was sitting—with a tiny dog snoring in his lap—it looked a little one-sided. His days were longer and far more physical than Heather's, and while he didn't begrudge her that—not really—right now, he couldn't help but wonder about how fair this setup really was.

She had an entire office staff at her disposal to help her... do what? Push papers around? Pay some bills? Meanwhile, he was getting sweaty and dirty and doing a shit-ton of grunt work. How was that a partnership?

Plus, she was out on a date with Randy!

"I'm being crazy, right?" he said to the dog. "I can't honestly expect Heather to walk onto a job site and start pulling down drywall, but..."

And that was just it. He didn't know. He wasn't sure what he wanted or what he expected of her, except that she not be off flitting around town with some guy while he was the one doing the majority of the work on putting Tom's mind at ease.

Tomorrow—yes, definitely tomorrow—he was going to talk to her about where she saw this business going. Was she just planning on riding the current wave of what her father had built, or was she looking and thinking of ways to improve and build the business?

It was about time he figured out just how useful of a partner he was going to be stuck with.

FIVE

The following Thursday, Heather felt like she was about to drown in paperwork.

She wasn't sure what had gotten into Chris this week.

It had started fairly reasonably. On Monday, he'd wanted her to write up a plan for her ideas on expanding and improving the business. She'd been thinking through all that for months now, and it was smart to have it written out, so she'd been happy to oblige. But after she'd given it to him on Wednesday—a very detailed and professional report—he'd demanded that she provide all this evidence in support of her ideas, pulling from the entire history of their previous jobs.

Those records, as Heather was all too aware, were kept in paper files in a tiny storage room in the basement, so she'd had to spend hours there pulling information and then trying to compile it all into a coherent form for Chris.

It crossed her mind that he was just being a jerk—giving her busywork just so she had to put even more effort into her job—but she hated to assume something like that, especially since he seemed to be making an attempt to spend time with her father and invest time and energy in the company.

Maybe he just really did want to do a good job.

She hoped so. But either way, she didn't have a choice but to collect all the information he asked for. She knew a challenge when she was offered one, and she wasn't going to let Chris get the better of her.

But her head was spinning from peering at so many old files, and she hadn't yet implemented a good computer system for keeping records, so she was compiling the information on PowerPoint spreadsheets.

On Thursday, she was only halfway done at six thirty in the evening, and she'd started at six o'clock that morning.

She was exhausted, and she had a headache, and she was mentally cursing Chris for demanding all this information. She'd worked late every night this week, and she'd had to cancel a lunch she'd scheduled with Randy yesterday. Not that she cared too much about the lunch, but it was the principle of the thing.

What the hell did Chris need all this for anyway? He'd never been a numbers guy. He was a hands-on, hammer-the-nail kind of guy.

She was scowling at the computer screen in the empty office—her father and Jenny, who answered the phones and helped out around the office, had left more than an hour ago—when a sound at the door startled her.

She looked up to see Chris coming in.

She was hard pressed to summon a smile. "What are you doing here?"

"I was checking to see if you had that stuff for me yet?"

She blinked. "Not yet. I'm still working on it." Surely he couldn't expect her to pull years' worth of information together from paper files in a couple of days. That would take a miracle.

He frowned. "How long do you think you'll need?"

Evidently he did think she could perform such a miracle. She frowned back at him. "I don't know. It's a huge amount of information. I can't just wave my wand and make it happen." She caught herself as her voice sounded too sarcastic.

She wasn't a sarcastic person normally. Normally, people would call her sweet and sincere. She wasn't sure why Chris always brought out this side of herself, but she wanted to rein it in as much as possible.

For one thing, they had to work and live together. For another, she didn't like to think he had the power to change her.

"I wasn't saying you should wave your wand. I just asked how long it would take."

She took a deep breath. "I'm not sure. I'd guess I'm about halfway through. Hopefully, I'll be done by early next week."

He was opening his mouth to reply when his phone rang, and after he checked the screen, he held up a hand to indicate he was answering it and he'd return to their conversation in a moment.

"Hey, Tom," he said after connecting the call. "What's up?"

She frowned, wondering what her father wanted from Chris this evening. Obviously it would be work related, and it probably wasn't important at all. But it bothered her that she couldn't tell the topic of conversation from Chris's commentary, which was made up of nothing but "Sounds good" and "Sure thing" and "Got it."

When he'd hung up, he turned back to face her. "Sorry about that."

"What did my dad want?"

He gave a half shrug. "Nothing. Just work stuff."

"What work stuff?"

"Why does it matter?"

Heather's frown deepened. "It doesn't matter. I just want to know. Why won't you tell me?"

Chris stared at her like she was a curious experiment. "Are you always this nosy?"

"I'm not nosy. But that's my father, and I'm part of this company. If it's work related, why can't I know?"

"He was just giving me some advice about the Garner job. The guys were having some trouble with the original woodwork."

Heather relaxed. "Oh."

Chris was still eyeing her like he was trying to figure her out. "You didn't think there was something going on behind your back, did you?"

"No," she admitted, feeling kind of silly about her reaction now. "It's just... secret conversations make me... really nervous."

"It wasn't secret." He'd come a little closer, and his expression had changed—like he wasn't just peering at her now, like he genuinely wanted to understand her.

"I know. But you wouldn't tell me, and I'm... irrationally sensitive about that kind of thing." She was a little embarrassed to tell him how horrified she'd been every time her parents had closed their bedroom door to fight when she was a child, not letting her hear what was going on. "Just leftovers from my parents' breakup."

"I get it," he murmured. "We all have those kinds of leftovers, I guess."

"Yeah." She gave him a little smile, feeling better.

He smiled back, and she felt like they understood each other for real in that moment.

Then his expression changed yet again, and he asked, "So when do you think you'll be done with this stuff?"

She gave a little jerk, like he'd flung sand in her eyes. All her softer feelings evaporated as she remembered his obnoxious pushiness. "It will be done when it's done. I'm working as hard as I can."

"All right then. No need to snap my head off."

Her tone had been a little cool, but she'd definitely not snapped. "I didn't snap your head off."

"Well, you snapped something off."

She scowled at him. "If you don't stop being annoying, I'm going to snap off something you like very much, and then how will you feel?"

He looked surprised by her comeback, and then he started to laugh.

He was still chuckling as he left the office.

He was a very good laugher, she had to admit. His whole face warmed in an incredibly attractive way. All kinds of things were attractive about him.

This morning, he'd come out of his room without a shirt on to get his coffee, and she'd almost melted at the sight of his gorgeous, masculine chest.

She'd wanted to touch it, touch him. She still did.

She brushed the thought away since it would do her absolutely no good.

She wasn't going to touch him. Not at all. Never.

She was a sensible woman, and she wasn't at the mercy of her occasional lustful urges.

She just had to remember that.

~

Later that evening, Heather was sprawled out on her chair in the apartment, staring at the television.

Chris had been in his room when she'd finally got home, which was a great relief. She didn't want to see him or talk to him. She'd warmed up some soup, since she didn't have energy to make anything more, and ate it while she watched a cooking show on TV.

Lucy was perched on her lap now, peering at her hopefully, wanting either attention, a walk, or a treat.

At the moment, the dog wasn't going to get any of those things. Heather was too tired to move.

If she'd been smarter, she would have paced out the work involved in Chris's project and not almost killed herself getting it done so quickly. It wasn't like it was really urgent. Chris could have waited a little longer.

But Heather had always been an overachiever, and she didn't like anyone to think she couldn't do her job.

That applied double to Chris.

She wondered if he was taking his role in the company as seriously as it seemed.

That would be nice—if he was. Maybe he wouldn't be walking out the door next month as she half expected him to.

Her dad would be utterly crushed if Chris walked out on him again.

When she heard a noise from the other side of the apartment, she turned her head. Her eyes widened dramatically when she saw Chris come out of his room.

He wore a pair of boxers and nothing else. And damn, his body was fine. She could see even more of it right now than she had this morning, and the effect on her own body was dramatic.

This evening she had an even harder time tearing her eyes away from the broad chest, long legs, strong thighs, flat abs.

"Sorry," he said, evidently noticing her staring. "I thought you'd be in your room. It's late."

"Is it past my bedtime?" Her tone was a little sharp, so she tempered it as she added, "I just hadn't made it to my room yet."

He shrugged and headed to the refrigerator, where he pulled out a bottle of water. Instead of returning to his room, he came a little closer to her. "You look beat."

"I am. My head is still swimming with all those paper files. I told Dad he should have converted to computer records about ten years ago, but he never listened to me."

"We can do it then."

"Yeah. That's the plan." She gave him a vague smile. "It doesn't help in collecting information at the moment, of course."

"I guess that was a big project I asked for."

She couldn't tell if he was teasing her or apologetic. Either way, at least he acknowledged the ridiculous amount of work he'd given her. "Uh, yeah. I can't wait for the weekend. I'm going to lay around and not move for hours at a time."

"Good plan. Unless you have another date, of course."

She'd been petting Lucy, who looked like she might jump over to dote on Chris at any moment, but she glanced over at Chris's face at his words. "Nothing definite."

Randy had mentioned something about the weekend, but she wasn't sure she was going to say yes. She liked him well enough, but she didn't want to go out with him two weekends in a row because that would start to feel serious.

She definitely didn't want to be serious about Randy anytime soon.

At the moment, she was still having trouble keeping her eyes off Chris's chest and legs.

"Did you date a lot in Charlottesville?" he asked.

She managed to tear her eyes from his chest and move them up to his face. He looked casually interested, like he was just making conversation and didn't really care about the answer.

There was no reason not to reply. "Eh. I went out casually pretty often."

"Nothing serious?"

"I dated one guy for three months and another guy for five. That was as serious as it got."

"Why is that?"

She widened her eyes. "What kind of question is that? It just never worked out to be any more serious."

"I figured you were the one who didn't want to get serious, and I was wondering why." He looked completely genuine—not like he was teasing her or trying to bait her.

She realized it was a real compliment he'd given her—that he assumed any guy she dated would want to be serious with her. "I don't know. They just weren't the right guys, I guess. When it got to the point of deciding whether it was going to be serious or not, I just couldn't... see myself with them long-term." She sighed, realizing she'd never really acknowledged this to herself before. "I guess it has something to do with my mom walking out. It's hard for me to trust that... that a relationship is going to last, that he's not going to just leave me eventually."

"Yeah," Chris murmured, leaning back in his recliner. He wasn't looking at her now. "I get that."

"What about you?" she asked, feeling vulnerable and not wanting it to be one-sided.

"What about me?"

"Have you been serious about anyone?" She knew he'd never been serious about any girls when he'd lived in Preston, but the three intervening years were a blank.

"Nah."

"Why not?"

He didn't answer for a long time, and she thought he wasn't going to reply at all. But then he finally said into the silence. "I guess I'm kind of the opposite."

"In what way?"

"I'm the one who leaves."

She'd known that about him. He'd done it to her father three years ago. "Why do you think you do that?"

He turned his head suddenly to meet her eyes. "Who's going to trust *me* to stick around?"

Her chest clenched at the dry words, and she understood something about him she hadn't known before.

They weren't really as different as she'd always assumed. Both of them lived with these self-fulfilling prophecies. What they expected to happen always did—and it might be partly because they didn't know to hope for anything else.

~

The next morning, Heather was staring at her computer screen again, trying to input numbers into her spreadsheet.

Chris was in the inner office, talking to her father. She really wished she knew what they were talking about.

It was silly to feel that way, but she always got a little nervous when Chris and her father talked privately. It made her wonder if they were keeping secrets from her.

Of course there were no secrets. She knew that rationally. But she always felt that little prickle of anxiety anyway.

Her father's office door was partly opened, but she was too far away to hear what they were talking about. She told herself not to be stupid and tried to focus on her work instead.

She wasn't going to work over the weekend—that would be going well beyond the call of duty since Chris didn't need this information for a real deadline—but she wanted to get as much as possible done today so it all wouldn't be waiting for her next week.

She looked up when she heard Jenny greet someone who had just walked into the office.

It was a man delivering two big boxes.

Jenny handled ordering supplies, so Heather didn't know what was in the boxes, but she figured they were probably office supplies. With this determined, she turned back to her spreadsheet.

"Heather?" The male voice caused her to turn back toward the front of the office, where the delivery man was approaching her. "I'd heard you were back in town."

Heather smiled and stood up as her eyes focused on the man's face, and she recognized Billy Watson, who had been in her class at school from kindergarten on. "Billy! How great to see you!"

They hugged briefly, and Heather was glad of the distraction from her tedious work. Billy had been one of those guys who were always around. Nice enough, but nothing special. But he'd grown into a decent-looking man, and Heather was always happy to see a familiar face.

They chatted for a few minutes, catching up on each other's lives. Then Billy said, "Hey, we should get together some time."

"Yes, of course. That would be great."

"What about this weekend? Are you busy?"

"I was planning to do as little as possible this weekend, but I could probably manage dinner."

"Tomorrow then?" Billy looked excited, as if he hadn't expected her to say yes to a date.

Heather wasn't sure why she wouldn't say yes. She liked him, and she needed to rekindle her social life, especially since she was spending far too much time thinking about her emotionally unavailable roommate. "Sure. I'm in Preston's Mill. Unit F."

"Great. I'll pick you up around six thirty, if that sounds good. We'll just do something casual."

Heather agreed to this plan and watched him as he left the office. When she turned around, she was startled to see Chris standing silently outside her father's door.

He must have heard at least part of the conversation.

"So much for your lazy weekend," he said, his expression unreadable.

Heather had no idea why she felt flustered. There was absolutely nothing wrong with going out on a date, no matter what she'd said to Chris the day before. "I'll still have plenty of time to be lazy."

"At this rate, you'll have dated every single guy in town before the month is out."

Heather narrowed her eyes at him, trying to figure out why he was being so snide. He was almost acting jealous.

It was probably just a male territorial thing. It was silly, and she wasn't going to let it bother her. She gave him a very sweet smile. "When I run out of eligible men in Preston, I'll have to start scouring the surrounding towns too."

Chris made a wordless sound as his only reply.

SIX

Two weeks later, Chris walked into the office and smiled. There sat Jenny and a girl from the temp agency that they'd hired to help transfer all those old files onto the computer, and that was it. Heather was now the proud occupant of her own office in the far back corner of the building.

Where eager-beaver delivery guys couldn't see her and ask her out on dates.

Damn Billy.

Not that it had helped much. Oh no. Not only had she gone out to dinner with Billy, but she'd done lunch a couple of times with Randy, and just two nights ago, Heather had gone to some food truck rodeo with Dave, the landscaper over at their condo.

Unbelievable.

Freakin' *Dave*.

Although, if he was being fair, he could admit that she had been putting in long hours, and he could see that she was pulling her weight. They were never going to be equals here in terms of the physical stuff, but she was dealing with more of the mental aspect with all the office and paperwork stuff.

And there was no way he wanted to deal with the paperwork end of the business. No thank you.

With a little spring in his step at the new office layout, he stopped by his own office, did a quick job of entering in his receipts for the day, and followed up with some emails to a potential new subcontractor and supplier he had met earlier in the day. Feeling good about the way things were going,

Chris got up and went to find Tom. He enjoyed the time they spent together daily talking about the progress on jobs and the things Chris was lining up for future prospects.

He waved to Tom as he walked into his office when he saw the older man was on the phone. He was going to turn and leave, but Tom held up his hand and motioned for Chris to sit and that he'd be done in a minute. Not a big deal.

Chris took a seat and looked at his friend. Something was off. He couldn't quite put his finger on it, but there was *something*. He looked worn out, and his voice was a little strained. Maybe he was just tired or was talking to someone that he didn't like, but in all the years Chris had known Tom, this was something he had never witnessed before.

Tom hung up the phone and looked at Chris with a weary smile. "How did things go today? Did the drywall show up on time?"

This was what they normally did—they talked shop. But right now it was the last thing on Chris's mind. "You feeling all right, Tom?"

Rather than answer right away, Tom leaned back in his big leather chair and sighed. "Just tired," he said, but it didn't sound convincing. "It's nothing."

"Tom—"

"Did we ever hear back from Connor on that lumber for the Madison job? If he can deliver at the cost he pitched to us, we should jump on it."

"Tom," Chris said a little more sternly. "Come on. Don't worry about drywall and lumber. You look like hell, and to be honest, you're freaking me out a little. Let me go and get Heather—"

"No!" Tom interrupted a little too quickly and then sighed again. "Okay. I'm just... I've got a pain that just... well, it won't go away."

"Okay... where? Abdominal? Head? Chest? Did you fall? Get hurt on one of the sites?"

Tom shook his head. "Chest pain. It's been on and off for a couple of hours now. I took some antacids, but it's not helping. I was going to call my doctor, but I got stuck on that call with my damn financial advisor and just kept hoping the pain would go away."

Chris stood and looked down at the older man. "You need to go to the emergency room. Now. When did this start?"

"After lunch," Tom said, his voice weak. "That's why I thought it was just something I ate, but now..."

"Tom, I'm not joking here. You can either let me drive you, or I'm calling an ambulance."

The two men stared at each other for several moments, and Chris knew there was no way in hell that he wasn't getting Tom to the hospital. He was just about to play his ace in the hole and get Heather in here when Tom stood up.

"Okay," Chris said with relief. "Come on. I'll drive you."

"Thank you," Tom replied. "Let me just—"

It was the last thing he said before he collapsed.

It was chaos after that. Chris screamed out for Heather while he was already calling 911 on his cell phone. Everyone in the office came running, and Chris thrust his phone at Jenny while he began to try to get Tom to come around. Heather was beside him, frantically crying out to her father to wake up, and all the while Chris silently prayed that they hadn't waited too long to do something.

He started to try CPR, but Tom was breathing so that didn't seem to be what was needed. Tom just wouldn't wake up. Finally, the rescue squad came through the door. Stepping aside immediately, he gently helped Heather to her feet and held her as they both watched helplessly as Tom was placed on oxygen, put on a stretcher, and wheeled out.

They worked together to get Heather's belongings so they could follow the ambulance to the hospital. Chris called out over his shoulder to Jenny to make calls and let people know where he was going to be and that they could reach him—and him only—on his cell. He didn't want anyone bothering Heather right now.

It didn't take long to get to the hospital, and Chris instinctively took control of the situation—although he held Heather's hand the entire time. The ER receptionist noted that they were there and promised to call them as soon as they had any information on Tom. It wasn't the answer he wanted, but he also knew it would be pointless to argue right now.

He led Heather to a quiet corner of the waiting room, and they both sat down. "Do you want something to drink?"

She shook her head.

"Something to eat? Maybe a snack? Did you eat lunch today?"

She shook her head, but her hand never left his.

He was pretty sure she wasn't aware of just how strong her grip was, but he might have some serious bone fractures if he didn't do something.

Soon.

Casually, he pulled his hand away and put his arm around her, tucking her head on his shoulder. It felt... nice. Kind of perfect, actually. It was beyond inappropriate to be thinking like that right now, but he couldn't help it. He rested his head against hers and struggled with what to say. If anything.

And that's when he felt it.

A tear. Then another. And another. All landing on him. Her slight frame trembled against him, and it almost gutted him.

"He's going to be all right," he said softly, gruffly. "He's strong and healthy, and we got him here in record time."

"That was the scariest thing I've ever seen," she whispered. "He looked so pale and so helpless. It's... he's never... I've never..."

"Shh...," he said, not wanting her to get herself worked up. "I'm just glad we were all there and that he wasn't alone."

She sat up and straightened, looking at him. "Was he all right before he collapsed or..."

Chris immediately told her about his conversation with her father. "He tried to downplay it, but we were getting ready to go." Guilt washed over him at how much time he might have cost Tom. Had he only insisted sooner, then maybe...

"You know how stubborn he is," she said and then resumed her position against him, her head resting on his shoulder again. "I know he doesn't take as good of care of himself as he should. I get on him for it all the time. But I don't know what I'll do if something happens to him, Chris. I can't lose him. He's all I have."

He shook his head, emotion clogging his throat. "You have me," he said, his voice rough. "I'm right here with you."

"It's not the same," she said, but there was no bitterness in her tone. "Ever since my mom left, my dad has been everything to me. He's been both my mother and my father. He's been my friend, my confidant, my champion. That's the only life I've ever known."

"That's a good life to have," he responded, hugging her a little closer. "You're very lucky that you have that relationship. I don't know a lot of people that do. And knowing your dad, I think he would have been that way even if your mom had stayed. He's just that kind of guy."

"Maybe. I know it just about killed him when she left, and he was struggling with his own emotions the whole time, but he always put me first. He would sit there and listen to me cry and try to understand how my mom could leave me. Me!" She gave a snort of disgust. "It didn't even occur to me back then that she had left him too."

"You were a kid, Heather. It's completely natural at that age to only see what immediately pertains to you."

She shrugged. "I know. And we talked about it when I was older, but... still. He's just such a huge presence, and to see him like that... on the floor... and..."

"Miss Carver? Mr. Dole?"

They both looked up at the doctor approaching them and immediately stood. "Yes?" Chris said and automatically gripped Heather's small hand in his.

"Please, let's sit down." He motioned back to the seats. "I'm Dr. Mallins, and I'm assigned to your father's care."

Heather squeezed Chris's hand. "How is he? Is he awake? Was it a heart attack?"

The doctor looked at her and gave her a small smile. He was an older man—in his sixties with gray hair and kind blue eyes. "He is awake, and we're running some tests now. From the initial EKG, we don't believe it's a heart attack. There's a blood test we can do to verify that as well. Now that he's awake and was able to tell us where the pain was exactly, I'm leaning toward a gallbladder attack. That's what we're looking at now with an ultrasound."

"When will you know for certain?" Chris asked, concern lacing his tone.

"We'll need a couple of hours, and we'll be observing him overnight as well."

"Can we see him?" Heather asked anxiously.

"Not right now. He's heading down to radiology for the ultrasound. Why don't the two of you go and grab something to eat, and maybe in two hours we'll have a room for him. I'll make sure you get to see him."

"But—" Heather began to protest.

"Thank you, Dr. Mallins," Chris quickly interrupted. "We'll do that."

With a curt nod, Dr. Mallins turned and walked away.

Heather pulled her hand from his and faced him. "Why did you do that? Maybe we could have gone back to see him sooner? Maybe I could have gone to radiology with him? He's all alone! Someone should be with him!"

Her voice was nearing hysteria, and Chris knew if he didn't put a stop to it now, she'd lose it in a matter of minutes. "That's enough," he said firmly and almost smiled when her mouth snapped shut and her eyes went wide. "The doctors need to do their jobs, and they don't need us back there getting in the way. Now he asked us to give him a couple of hours, and we need to respect that."

And then her eyes began to well with tears.

With a muttered curse, he immediately pulled her into his arms and held her as she cried.

~

It was after midnight when they finally arrived home. Both were exhausted and quiet as they walked in. Lucy was near frantic and Heather immediately scooped her up and apologized profusely for being home so late.

"I'm so sorry, sweet girl," she cooed. "Let's get your leash."

"I'll take her," Chris said and walked over to the hook near the door and got the dog's leash.

"What? Why?"

"You're tired. It's been a long day. Why don't you go and get ready for bed, and I'll take care of Lucy. She'll need to eat too, and I'm not sure I'm ready to go to sleep yet so I'll stay up with her."

"Chris."

At the sound of his name on her lips like that, without thinking, he walked over to kiss her, catching himself at the last minute and pressing a light kiss on her head before getting the dog hooked up and walking out the door. Thankfully, Lucy was quick to do her business and they were back inside in less than five minutes. He unhooked her and then went over to the kitchen to put food and fresh water in her bowls before opening the refrigerator and pulling out a beer. He held it in his hands and decided it wasn't what he wanted and put it back before grabbing a bottle of water.

Behind him, he heard Heather moving around in the bathroom—no doubt washing her face and brushing her teeth. All the things that went into her nightly routine.

She'd been quiet on the ride home. They both were. It had taken a little over two hours after they'd first talked to Dr. Mallins before they were able to go up and see Tom. He was sedated and barely knew they were there, but Heather had sat at his side and talked to him for hours while Chris had gone out and talked with the doctor.

"As far as we can see, this isn't a cardiac event. We've done all the tests, and his heart is fine. His blood work is good."

"Then what's the problem?" Chris asked, raking a hand through his hair in frustration. "A healthy man doesn't collapse like that!"

"We saw gallstones in the ultrasound. They're fairly common, but when they go on the move, they're quite painful. We'll be removing his gallbladder in the morning. He's scheduled for tomorrow at eleven in the morning."

Chris had sagged with relief, and when he'd told Heather, she had been equally relieved. When he finally convinced her to leave, she had only agreed because Tom was sound asleep. She'd vowed to be back there first thing in the morning. There was no way Chris was going to argue with that or remind her that her car was still at the office and she'd have to rely on him to get there.

Lucy's bark brought him back to the present.

"You ready to go out again?" he asked with a chuckle, and the dog pranced back over to the door. Putting her leash back on, they repeated their path down the stairs and outside where Lucy was a little slower to do her business. Chris wanted to be annoyed, but he figured the poor dog had suffered enough with them coming home so late and being locked inside all day. And as much as he hated to admit it, she was a good dog.

Not that he was going to admit that to anyone anytime soon.

Or ever.

Looking down, he saw that she was finally taking care of business. Kicking her back paws behind her as she finished, she gave a little hop and turned back toward the building. "Good girl," he said and then wanted to roll his eyes.

Damn dog.

They were back in the apartment, and Chris hung her leash back up and locked the door. He was finally starting to relax. Maybe a little late night TV would help, but he knew if he got comfortable on Flo that he wouldn't make it to bed. He had a television in his room, but it wasn't quite the same as sitting on Flo.

Mentally, he began a running list of all the things that would need to be addressed in the morning with all the crews. There were going to be calls to make and decisions to be made on how long he could afford to be away from the sites. Tomorrow was a given. There was no way he was going to send Heather to the hospital alone. Even though it was routine surgery, and Dr. Mallins assured them Tom would come home the following day, it still wasn't right to make her go alone.

He'd call Jenny and see about getting a housekeeper or home health person to stay with Tom for a couple of days and...

"Hey."

Chris shook his head to clear it when he heard Heather's soft voice. She was standing in the doorway to her bedroom, wearing a pair of flannel boxers and a tank top. Her hair was loose, and she didn't have on a stitch of makeup. She looked young and sweet and... scared. He walked closer.

"How are you doing? You going to be able to sleep?"

She shrugged. "Physically, I think I will, but my brain won't quite shut down yet."

He nodded. "I know the feeling. I was just standing there thinking of the calls I'll need to make in the morning and all the things we'll need to handle to keep things going at work."

"Me too. There's so much going on at the office with the new software and converting the files. I can spare a day or two—especially for Dad—but I know it will stress him out more that I'm not at work. We'll have to ask at the hospital about referrals for a home health aide or something."

He chuckled.

"What?" she asked.

"I was just thinking the same exact thing," he said with a lopsided grin. Then he yawned. Loudly.

"Great minds," she said softly. Then she surprised him by reaching out and touching his arm. "Thank you."

He looked at her curiously. "For what?"

"For being there. For me and Dad. I... I don't know what I would have done without you."

Reaching up, he caressed her cheek. "You would have been fine. You're stronger than you think."

She smiled. "Still, I'm really glad you were there with me."

They stood there like that for a long minute—her hand on his arm, his caressing her cheek. He marveled at how soft her skin was and how small she looked. Delicate.

"Heather," he murmured, his head leaning toward hers as if an invisible chord was pulling him that way.

Her lips parted as she moved a little closer.

She smelled good. A light, floral scent hit him as he carefully wrapped his other arm around her waist, effectively closing the distance between them. And then he did what he'd been aching to do since the first day she walked through the apartment door.

He kissed her.

SEVEN

The kiss started gently, his lips lightly brushing against hers as if he were testing to see how it felt.

When a surge of excitement and pleasure rose inside her, she made a little noise in her throat and raised her hand to the back of his neck. Chris immediately deepened the kiss, slipping his tongue into her mouth.

She'd experienced plenty of good kisses in her life, but this was on a whole different level. Her head spun, and her body pulsed, and a deep need inside her sprang to life— one she'd never known she possessed.

Chris seemed to sense her response because his body was tightening and his hands were becoming more possessive. He slid them down her back, and one of them lowered to cup her bottom, pressing her more snugly against him. She clenched one of her hands in his shirt and held on, kissing him as eagerly as he was her.

When she felt a sharp tug of arousal, it was followed by a cold sliver of fear.

What the hell was she doing? Yes, he'd been great today, but she usually didn't even really like Chris. She absolutely shouldn't be kissing him this way, no matter how much her body and her heart clearly wanted it.

She broke her mouth away and gasped, "Wait. Chris, wait."

He froze for a moment, and then he released her with a low groan.

Heather took a quick step back. "What are we doing?" She wiped a hand against her mouth, as if that might somehow clear the aftermath of that amazing kiss from her mind. "What are we doing?"

"Kissing." His voice was slightly rough—as if he were affected by their embrace too—but he sounded more controlled than she felt. He took a step closer, his eyes hot with obvious interest. "And I wouldn't mind doing it again."

She could barely resist that look in his eyes, but the anxiety coursing through her was enough to prompt her to raise her hand to stop his approach. "I don't think we should."

He let out a breath. "Why not? It was good."

"Yes. It was good. But that doesn't mean it's a good idea."

"Why not?"

"Because we're both—not ourselves this evening."

She was trying desperately to be reasonable and smart, but the sight of him standing in front of her, big and handsome and bristly from a day's worth of beard, looking at her like he wanted to swallow her whole, was almost more than she could handle. In about five seconds, she was going to be back in his arms, giving herself to him completely.

"I think we're ourselves," Chris said slowly.

"Well, I'm not. I've got to…" What she had to do— right now, as quickly as she could—was get away from him. "I've got to… go to bed. We can talk in the morning."

She whirled around and hurried into her room, closing the door behind her.

She leaned against it, breathing deeply. Yes, that had been a cowardly retreat, but her only other choice would be to surrender to her highly inappropriate feelings.

She probably would have had sex with him if he'd continued deepening the embrace. She wasn't sure she would have had the will or brains to stop them, since it was becoming clear that she wanted it so much.

That would have been a huge mistake.

At least she'd saved herself from *that*.

She jumped at a knock on her door, right behind her.

"Heather?" Chris's voice was low, still hoarse.

"Sorry," she said through the door, praying that he would listen to her, not keep pushing on this. "I'm really sorry, but we need to talk in the morning. I'm... I'm not myself, and I don't want to do something I'll regret."

"Heather?" he repeated.

"I... I really think it's for the best."

Silence.

Maybe he was finally going away.

"Look... can you just open the door? Just for a second?"

She groaned, knowing if she opened the door and looked at him again that there was a good chance she'd fling herself back into his arms. "Can't we just—"

"Heather." This time her name was a near growl.

With a sigh of defeat, she opened the door just a couple of inches. But before she could even look at him, his hand shot through the opening—with Lucy on it. Her tongue was lolling and her tail was wagging, and she looked excited to be part of this ridiculous situation.

Oh. So he hadn't wanted to talk to or kiss her again. She reached up and took Lucy—careful to not touch Chris's hand.

She cleared her throat but couldn't seem to make herself say anything.

There was a longish pause. Then, "Okay. Talk to you tomorrow."

"Thank you," she called, relieved and now wanting him even more. A lot of guys would have been pushy, just ignoring her wishes and demanding to be let in. "Good night."

When she heard him retreating and then the muffled sound of his bedroom door closing, she let out a long sigh and walked over to slump onto her bed. What a mess. She'd been needy and vulnerable, and she'd let down her guard far too much.

Chris wasn't a bad guy. Now that she'd gotten to know him again, he was a lot better than she'd been thinking. He was fine for this roommating thing and even for being a business partner with, for as long as he wanted to stick around.

But he wasn't a committer. She'd learned that the hard way a few years ago.

She needed stability. She was at the point in her life when she was looking toward the future, toward building a good life for herself. And the most stupid thing she could do was fall for a guy who wasn't going to be around for the long haul.

She'd just been upset about her father tonight. That was all that had happened. People sometimes kissed someone they didn't intend to, and it wasn't the end of the world.

That was all that had happened tonight.

She really hoped her dad was okay.

Her phone rang just then, as if her thoughts had conjured the sound. She gasped when she saw the caller was her father.

"Dad!" she said after scrambling to connect the call. "You're supposed to be sleeping."

"I was," he replied, sounding weak but still with his characteristic dry intelligence. "But they keep coming in, checking on me every other minute, and I kept worrying about you."

"Why are you worried about me?" she asked, her voice breaking slightly. "You're the one in the hospital. You're the one having surgery tomorrow."

"I'm okay."

"No, you're not. Are you in a lot of pain?"

"Nah. They've doped me up pretty good. How are you holding up, Heather?"

"I'm fine. Why wouldn't I be?"

"Well, I did have some vague thoughts about you there by yourself, falling apart."

She sniffed and smiled. "I'm not falling apart."

"Is Chris with you?"

"He's in the apartment," she said slowly. "He lives here."

"I know that. I mean is he helping you out? You need to have someone with you."

"I'm fine, Dad. I really am. Chris is helping out. We're going to cover everything at work while you're in the hospital, and I'll be there first thing tomorrow so I can see you before you go into surgery."

"Okay. Good. Sorry about all this."

She almost choked. "Don't be ridiculous! You can't apologize for health problems, Dad."

"I'm your dad. I can do what I want."

She started to laugh, but it turned into a little sob before she knew what was happening. It was a moment before she could say coherently, "Yes, you can. You're going to be just fine. Now get some sleep so you're ready for tomorrow."

"So Chris is there?"

She felt weird that her father was taking comfort in that, but she also didn't want to take that comfort away. "Yes, he's here. I'm doing fine."

"Good. Good. You need someone." His voice was fainter, like he was getting tired.

"Good night, Dad," she said softly. "I'll see you in the morning."

When she'd hung up, she stared at the phone for a minute before she finally put it down.

Her dad was right about one thing. She did need someone. The idea of his dying—sometime in the future, hopefully in the very-far-off future—was like a huge dark void, threatening to consume her.

She would have no real family then—no family that acted like family, anyway.

She'd always kind of assumed she'd be married with her own family by the time her father died. He'd been a healthy man all his life, so she was hoping he'd have a good long life. But today had really scared her.

What if she ended up completely alone when he died?

The thought was terrifying—so scary she couldn't let herself dwell on it. Her father was okay. He wasn't going to die anytime soon. She had time. Plenty of time.

But she definitely couldn't let herself wander down a dead-end road with a guy who would never commit to her and give her what she needed.

Chris was hot. No question about that. And he was funny and smart and could be surprisingly kind. But he ran away when life got hard, and that just didn't work for her.

She'd been needy tonight, so she'd kissed him, but she absolutely couldn't let it go any further than that.

No more kissing. No more soft thoughts about him.

They were roommates and business partners. And they could be friendly.

But absolutely nothing else.

~

Heather didn't sleep very well.

After a couple of hours tossing in bed, worrying about everything, she finally took a couple of antihistamines, which always knocked her out. She went to sleep after that, but she woke up when her alarm went off, groggy and fuzzy-headed.

She rolled out of bed and had to stand for a minute to fight off a wave of dizziness.

Too much had happened yesterday. She couldn't process it all. And today her dad was going to have surgery.

It was just six in the morning, but she wanted to get over to the hospital early so she could sit with her dad for a little while before they took him into pre-op.

She went to the bathroom and then was about to head to the kitchen for coffee when she caught a glimpse of herself in the mirror. She was still wearing the tank and boxers she'd slept in, and they left a lot of her body uncovered.

If Chris wasn't up now, he would be soon. She grabbed a robe to pull on over her pajamas so she'd be more covered up if she saw him.

After last night, she needed to be a lot more careful.

She was pouring herself a cup of coffee when Chris's bedroom door opened. Like her, he headed first for the bathroom, so she just caught a glimpse of a broad, bare chest and a pair of black sweatpants before the door closed.

She was leaning against the counter, sipping her coffee, when he came out of the bathroom and headed toward her in the kitchen. While she was tempted to try to avoid him this morning, she wasn't going to do that.

The mature, reasonable thing to do was have a conversation this morning about the kiss, so that was what she was going to do.

"Morning," he said, his voice slightly rough from sleep. Very sexy. So was the sight of his strong, masculine chest and broad shoulders.

"Good morning," she said with a little smile.

"Hear anything from your dad?" He leaned over briefly to greet Lucy, who had run up to him excitedly.

"He called last night. He sounded okay. They had him on pain medicine, so he was comfortable enough. Hopefully the procedure today will go smoothly, and he'll be on his way to recovery."

"Yeah." Chris nodded as he filled his mug and brought it to his lips. "Good."

She recognized that his eyes were on her face, watching her discreetly. He was wondering about the kiss, about her reaction to it. She felt her cheeks warming as she remembered how eager and passionate she'd been after the slightest touch of his lips.

Better to get it over with right away so things could go back to normal between them.

"About last night," she began, her voice cracking slightly because she was nervous about bringing it up.

Chris turned his head to meet her eyes. "Yeah?"

"I was... really scared about my dad, so I was needy, and... and I made a mistake."

He narrowed his eyes slightly. "I'm the one who kissed you."

"I know. But I kissed you back, and I shouldn't have. I was really needy." She'd already said that. She hated sounding so incoherent, but she wished Chris would stop looking at her like that, like he was trying to read her mind. "It was a good kiss," she began.

"Yeah. I know it was." His eyes flared up briefly, as if he was remembering exactly how good it was.

That wasn't what she wanted to talk about. Or remember. She cleared her throat. "So obviously there's some... some attraction between us. But we can't act on it."

"Why not?"

"Because..." She didn't want to tell him that she knew he would never commit to her. It might hurt his feelings, and she didn't want to do that. She also vaguely knew that normal girls weren't even thinking about commitment at this point, and she didn't want him to think she was even more high maintenance and uptight than he already did. In a flurry of confusion and anxiety, she managed to say, "Because it's not what I want. I only kiss guys that I want relationships with, and that's... that's never going to work with you."

There. That was the truth. It wasn't the whole truth, but it was as much as she could give him.

Chris might want to kiss her again. He might want to do much more. But he wasn't going to want a serious relationship with her, so just the hint of it should scare him off pretty effectively.

"Oh," he said, after blinking once. "Right. Of course."

She let out a breath. "I don't want things to get weird between us since we have to work together and live together for five more months. So—so are we okay?"

His expression cleared. "Yeah. Of course we are. No more kissing."

She scanned his face. She couldn't really see the realness she sometimes saw in his expression, but he didn't look offended or angry or annoyed, so he must be okay with things. "No more kissing. Good."

It didn't actually sound good. That kiss had been so amazing it was sort of depressing to know it would never happen again. But her mind was working at full capacity now, and she knew this was the best thing for her.

She just couldn't let herself explore this particular road—no matter how tantalizing it seemed at the moment. This road would never go where she needed it to go.

"So you're going to spend the day at the hospital?" Chris asked, clearly making an effort to change the subject and get back to a normal tone between them.

"Yeah," she said, relaxing as she accepted that this was going to be *them* from now on.

"I can go with you. You shouldn't have to wait there alone."

This sweet thought almost undid her resolute attitude, but she fought through it. "Thanks, but I'll be all right. I think Dad would rather someone be at work, making sure things get covered. I'm going to the hospital early, and I'm planning to stay most of the day."

"I'll take care of everything. I can drop you back at work this morning to pick up your car. I might stop by the hospital after he's awake and back in his room just so I can say hello and see how's he's doing." He slanted her a quick look. "If that's all right with you."

"Sure. Definitely. My dad will be really glad to see you." She smiled at him, feeling a little quiver of concern. "We're okay, aren't we? The two of us, I mean? Things have been going pretty well, so I don't want them to get weird."

"They won't get weird." He smiled at her, and it looked sincere, more like his normal self, which made her sigh in relief. "No sense in rocking the boat, since we're stuck in it together."

She actually laughed. "Okay. I've got to get dressed and get going. I'll give you a call when they take him into surgery and then keep you updated on how he's doing."

"Thanks."

When she went back into the bathroom, she felt better.

Her father was going to be fine.

And things with Chris were going to be fine.

And she could definitely live the rest of her life without a kiss like the one they'd shared last night.

After all, kissing wasn't the most important thing in the world.

EIGHT

"You know... just because I'm on a restricted diet doesn't mean that *you* have to be," Tom said a week later when Chris went to see him. Tom was sipping some hot tea, and Chris opted for the same.

Shrugging, Chris said, "It's not really a big deal. And it's not all that bad."

"It's not coffee with three sugars and half-and-half either," Tom countered and then sighed as he tried to get comfortable in his chair. "How are the jobs going? Tell me something to get my mind off the fact that I have five incisions in my abdomen and all I want is a bacon cheeseburger."

Chris chuckled. "So you're having some food withdrawals."

"That would be an understatement."

For the next fifteen minutes, Chris gave him the status of each of their current jobs and what was on the agenda to bid on over the next week.

"It sounds like you've got everything under control," Tom said, looking and sounding pleased.

Even before Tom had gotten sick, there was something Chris had wanted to discuss with him. But with the hectic schedule and trying to get settled in—both on the job and at home with Heather—there hadn't been time. Now on a peaceful Tuesday evening, it seemed like he'd finally have his chance.

"Tom?"

"Uh-oh," Tom quickly interrupted. "I don't like that tone. It sounds serious."

Chris couldn't help but smile. "It is. But not in a bad way. At least, I don't think it is."

"Oh. Okay."

"I don't think I've thanked you properly for offering me this opportunity." He paused and stared into his mug, since conversations like this had always made him uncomfortable. "I was a little shocked when you called me about it. I mean we hadn't talked much since I left, but—"

"Chris, I know you had your reasons for leaving. It wasn't personal."

"No... no. I know it wasn't," he replied. "And I know it wasn't exactly the first time I sort of... took off..."

"You were a kid, Chris. And if memory serves, you'd disappear for a day or two. But you always came back and you never missed a day of work. Scared your mother a bit though."

He nodded, remembering. "I know. I don't know how she put up with me."

"Parents put up with a whole hell of a lot and love you no matter what. At least, that's what good parents normally do. It's not easy—some of you make it harder than others—but in the end, we're quick to forgive."

"Yeah, well, I wish everyone was quick to forgive and understand."

"Understand what?"

"That leaving wasn't about anyone other than me. It was my issue. No one else's."

"Oh, I don't think anyone thinks that."

"Heather does."

Tom chuckled. "Well, my daughter has a lot of ideas about a lot of things. You don't have to always agree with her. Has she been giving you grief about it?"

Now it was Chris's turn to laugh. "Not as much as when I first got back." He shrugged. "I just... I want you to know that it wasn't an easy decision for me to make. My mother was all that I had, and the thought of being here without her—without any family—was just a little too much to handle."

"I always thought that we were like family, Chris. You've always been like a son to me. Working with you and teaching you about building and carpentry was an honor for me. You were a quick study, and you always took pride in your work. And for that, I was proud of you."

Looking up, Chris gave Tom a sad smile. "I let you down. I didn't talk to you about it. I made a rash decision and left you in a lurch. That wasn't right or fair, and it was disrespectful on my part. Heather's right that I didn't treat you right. At all. I'm sorry for that."

"Like I said, I knew you had your reasons." Tom took a sip of his tea before speaking again. "That's not to say that I wasn't disappointed that you didn't come to me with your struggles. I would have helped. I may not have had all the answers, but I would have been there for you—no matter what you would have decided. That's what friends do for one another."

"I didn't understand what it was like to trust another adult that way," Chris responded sadly. "And the memories... they were just too hard."

"And how has it been since you got back?"

"I've kept busy," Chris admitted. "I'm not going to lie. I drove by my old house, and I've gone to the cemetery every week and brought Mom flowers. I apologized to her too for skipping out the way I did."

They sat in silence for several long moments, each lost in their own thoughts before Tom spoke.

"Let me ask you something."

"Anything."

"What did you learn from your time away?"

Chris looked at him with confusion.

"I'm serious," Tom added. "I'm not looking for the politically correct answer, and I'm not looking for you to blow smoke up my ass. I seriously want to know what life taught you while you were gone."

"Honestly? I learned to be independent," he began, surprised by the question and by the fact that he was answering so openly. "I worked hard—sometimes too hard. There were times when I was up for days because I needed to prove that I could. Then I learned to not be so hard on my damn self." He paused. "I used every skill you taught me, and I used them to teach others how to do shit right. But at the end of the day, my life was empty."

Tom nodded with understanding. "And how do you feel now? Now that you're back?"

Chris gave him a slow smile. "I don't feel empty. I feel like I have a purpose. I take pride in the jobs we're doing—and it's not the same as the jobs I worked on for the past three years. Those I did and did what I was supposed to and then left. But here? Here I just feel... I don't know... a connection."

And now Tom smiled. "Because there's a pride that goes with ownership."

Chris shook his head. "No. It's not just that it's... this is my home town. And this is your business, and I want..."

His voice was suddenly thick with emotion. "I want to make you proud, and I want to do right by the reputation you earned for quality work. I don't want to let you down."

"You could never do that, son," Tom said. "And if it didn't hurt so damn much to lean forward, I'd clap you on the back. But I can't—just know that I want to."

"Noted," Chris said, straightening in his seat and finishing his drink. He placed the mug down on the coffee table and smiled. "I'm serious, Tom. I want this business to stay strong and grow even stronger. I'm not going to let you down."

"You couldn't, Christopher. I always knew that. That's why you're here. But I want you to remember one very important thing."

"What's that?"

"Don't make it your entire life. Make time for yourself and remember to let people in."

"There's a lot to do right now, Tom. I don't have a whole lot of time to socialize."

"Change that. I know Heather's been going out. She's had a couple of dates since she moved back."

Like Chris needed to be reminded of that.

"As a matter of fact, she's going out with... oh, what's that guy's name?"

"Dave," Chris muttered, almost missing the pleased look on Tom's face.

"That's right. Dave. We've used him a couple of times on jobs that required landscaping. He does great work."

Well, Dave wouldn't be getting hired on any of Chris's jobs, that was for sure.

"She said they were going to a movie tomorrow night." Tom smiled and nodded. "I'm glad she's getting out. And it's nice that she's dating a local boy."

"Dave's hardly a boy, Tom."

"Still. You know what I mean. You should find yourself a nice girl to date. Take her to dinner, go dancing or maybe just, you know, to a movie."

Wait… was Tom trying to tell him something? When he looked up, Tom wasn't looking at him, but he certainly had an amused look on his face.

Huh.

Maybe it was time to go out and dip his feet back in the dating pool.

~

"Hey, I hate to ask this—again—but would you be able to feed Lucy and take her out a couple of times tonight?"

Heather was scurrying around the apartment, getting ready for her date. She wasn't looking in Chris's direction, or she might have noticed that he was busy getting himself ready to go out.

"No can do, sweet pea," he said pleasantly. "I've got plans."

She stopped and looked at him, blinking twice before speaking again. "Plans?"

He nodded, trying not to look smug. "Yup. A date."

"A date?"

"That's right," he said in a teasing, singsong voice. "So as much as I'd love to help you, I'm afraid Lucy is on her own tonight."

"Oh, well, I guess that's okay."

She looked more than a little flustered and confused, but adorable as hell. "Which part—Lucy being on her own or me having a date? Because I'm pretty sure I didn't have to ask permission before going out."

"Lucy," she snapped, "I meant Lucy." And then the poor dog thought she was getting yelled at and quickly ran to her bed and hid her face.

"Now look what you've done," Chris admonished. "You upset her."

"I did not. You did!"

"I'm not the one who yelled at her," he reminded her, sounding as cool and reasonable as he could be.

"I didn't... I just..." Heather growled with frustration as she walked across the room, cooing at Lucy.

Chris left them to it while he walked back to his room to grab his wallet and keys. He wasn't sure if he was looking forward to this date or not. It had been fairly easy to arrange. Janet, who worked for the building supply company over on Mason Street, had been dropping hints for weeks that she'd love to go out with him. So when he went in to pick up a small order of two-by-fours today, he'd asked her to dinner. He knew it was short notice, but she didn't seem to mind.

So now they were going to dinner.

He just hoped he remembered how to make small talk and not curse like a sailor or talk shop all night.

Damn pressure.

With his keys and wallet in hand, he strode from the room and toward the front door. "Have a good night!"

"I will," Heather replied.

And because he just couldn't resist, he turned and said, "I was talking to Lucy."

~

He was bored.

Utterly and completely bored.

Janet was nice enough but... boring. Not that she hadn't openly hinted that she'd be fine just going back to her place and showing him her... whatever. But he wasn't interested.

And that just pissed him off.

They were halfway through their dinner when movement by the front door caught his eye.

Heather and Dave.

Son of a bitch!

Why? Why were they here? Weren't they supposed to go to a movie? Isn't that what Tom had said? So then why... Then it hit him like a ton of bricks. Dinner and a movie. Typical date stuff.

The restaurant was packed. He and Janet hadn't even ordered yet, and they were seated at a table big enough for four. There was only one way to salvage this bad date, and that was to have a little fun.

He was hit with a brainstorm on how to do just that.

"Hey," he said, interrupting Janet's running dialogue about the cost of birch versus pine. "That's Heather over there by the door and her date, Dave. Why don't we ask them to join us?"

Janet looked over toward the door and looked at Chris suspiciously. "Isn't she your boss?"

Well, damn. That irked. "No. She's Tom's daughter. And I told you about his emergency surgery, didn't I? The poor kid's been a nervous wreck all week. I think she's just out with Dave to take her mind off her dad's failing health."

"Failing health? I thought it was just his gallbladder."

"You know how these things go, Janet. It starts out as something small, and the next thing you know... BAM!"

Her eyes went wide. "What? What's bam?"

Hell, what was bam? He wondered. "You know... something... bigger. Come on, you don't want Heather sitting there thinking about her dad dying, do you?"

"Well, I guess not."

He jumped up from the table and excused himself.

"Hey! Fancy seeing you here!" He approached Heather and Dave, waiting to be seated. "Looks like there's a long wait here tonight."

"That it does," Dave replied. "I didn't think we'd need reservations."

Chris almost rolled his eyes. This was a chain restaurant. They didn't take reservations. Jerk. "Look, Janet and I just got seated a little while ago—"

"But you left like an hour ago," Heather said.

Chris nodded. "The line was that long." Then he shook his head. "I sure hope you had nothing else planned tonight."

"We're supposed to see a movie," Dave replied. "Maybe we should go someplace else."

"That would be—"

"Nonsense," Chris quickly interjected. "We have room at our table. Why don't you join us?"

"Are you sure?" Dave asked, smiling.

Heather, on the other hand, looked less than amused. "Yeah, Chris," she said dryly. "Are you sure?"

"Of course! What could be better than dinner out with friends?"

"I can think of a few things," Heather murmured as they made their way toward the table.

Chris slid into his side of the booth—because he'd already been sitting there with his drink—and waited to see where Heather and Dave would end up. Dave slid in next to him, Heather next to Janet.

All in all, it wasn't so bad. They laughed and ordered dinner, and the conversation flowed perfectly. Well, almost perfectly. He made sure that he and Dave and Janet had a lot to talk about—things about job sites and materials—while Heather didn't have much to contribute to the conversation.

When Dave excused himself to go to the men's room, Chris looked at Heather and grinned. "Your boyfriend's a great guy. And he knows so much about landscape materials."

She merely stared at him with a tight smile and practically dove for the check when it arrived.

"What's the hurry?" Chris asked.

"We have a movie to get to."

"Ooh! A movie!" Janet said with delight. "That sounds like fun. Chris, we should go too!"

His thoughts exactly.

By the time Dave got back to the table, things were already in motion, and he seemed equally pleased for them to be continuing with their double date.

"We'll meet you over there," Chris said.

"Nah, the parking is going to be crazy. It's such a small lot. Goes with the whole one tiny theater in town when there's a new movie out. You can just ride with us."

"That's not really necessary," Heather argued lightly, but no one was listening. Within minutes, they were all seated in Dave's SUV and heading across town to the theater.

"So we're seeing that new Western, right?" Chris asked.

"No," Heather interrupted. "We're seeing the romantic comedy."

"Oh, well that's too bad. Because I heard the Western—"

"Is not what we're seeing." she quickly cut in.

"I didn't think you were serious, Heather," Dave said, glancing over at her as he drove. "I mean, I guess it's not the worst thing to see but I'm with Chris on this one. I'd really like to see the Western."

If he could have high-fived himself without looking like a complete ass, Chris would have done it.

They made it across town, parked, had their tickets in hand, and were walking into the theater in no time. Janet tried to hold his hand, but Chris didn't want to lead her on. Better to keep it casual. He already knew they weren't going to go on a second date, so he wanted to at least be decent about it.

As they made their way to their seats, Chris felt like he was stuck in a time warp. The theater was tiny, and although there were two screens in the building, each theater was small and out of date, carrying movies released several months earlier. He thought about some of the massive multiplex theaters he'd seen while he traveled and couldn't help but wonder how Preston had stayed behind the times. Although, as he looked around, he noted how the building would benefit from a historical-style rehab. Maybe they'd have to look into that.

He turned to mention it to Heather, but she was glaring at him.

As she had been for the past eighty-seven minutes.

They found seats and—as it turned out—he ended up sitting next to Heather. "What do you think about a rehab on this place?" he whispered.

"What do you think about going to hell?" she replied pleasantly.

"Aww, don't be mad. I'm sure you'll enjoy this movie just as much as that chick flick. You want some popcorn?"

Heather looked at him like he was crazy. She looked at Dave and then Janet. Then to her lap and back at Chris. "Do you see any popcorn here?"

He rolled his eyes. "I meant that I was going to get some and was asking if you wanted any too. Sheesh. Unclench."

"Un…," she sputtered to say something else, but he simply patted her hand and stood up.

"Believe it or not, I know we just finished dinner, but I can't watch a movie without popcorn. Anyone interested?"

Dave was just about to answer when his cellphone rang. He held up a hand to them and Chris turned to Janet. "You want anything? Soda? Candy?"

But she was looking over at Dave. "Um, no. I'm good."

He shrugged, stepped around her, and went out to the lobby and bought their largest bucket of popcorn, a Coke and a box of Sno-Caps. Everyone liked them, right? With his arms full, he made his way back to his seat and noticed that Dave was still on the phone, Janet was texting on her phone, and Heather was looking extremely peeved at the whole situation.

"Snow Cap?" he asked, shaking the box in her direction after he sat down.

"No, thank you."

He turned to Janet, but she declined too.

The lights went down, and Dave excused himself to go finish his call. So Chris was left sitting between Heather and Janet and was suddenly not feeling so comfortable. Janet had noticeably started leaning away from him—as did Heather—and he had enough junk food to feed all four of them, but no one was eating.

Fan-freaking-tastic.

The movie started, and then Chris forgot all about the ridiculous situation and let himself get sucked into the story. He noticed that after a little while, Dave had come back and Heather was sharing his popcorn. Two hours later, when it was over, they all stood and stretched. The popcorn was long gone, his drink was empty, but the Sno-Caps remained. Not a big deal, he thought. They certainly wouldn't go to waste.

Heather was quiet as they walked out. Janet had enjoyed the movie and was talking about it, a lot.

With Dave.

What the…

It didn't matter. If anything, it made things a little less awkward right now. They climbed back into Dave's SUV and returned to the restaurant where Chris was parked.

"Look, maybe this is a bit… strange," Dave said, "but it would probably be easier if I took Janet home and the two of you went together since, you know, you live together."

"You live together?" Janet cried. "You never mentioned that!"

"It's not what you think," both he and Heather replied at the same time, but then neither bothered to explain. What was the point?

In minutes, they were climbing out of Dave's SUV. Janet thanked Chris for a nice night but made no mention of doing it again. And from what he could hear, Dave wasn't asking for another date either.

They stood and watched Dave and Janet drive off before Chris shrugged and began to walk over to his truck. He had it unlocked and the door open before he realized Heather hadn't followed.

"What's wrong?" he asked.

She didn't answer.

He sighed wearily. "Come on, Heather," he began. "We should get home. Lucy's probably dying to go out." He knew that the mention of her dog would get her to move.

And it did.

They drove in silence. Weird, tense silence. The kind of silence that made you dread what was going to happen next.

By the time they were back at the apartment, Chris didn't even wait for her. He made his way inside, up the stairs, and down the hall—thankful that Estelle was probably asleep—and straight to their door. Sure enough, Lucy was dancing around anxiously, and rather than wait for Heather, he grabbed her leash and made his way back down the stairs, passing Heather along the way, who didn't even stop to acknowledge the dog.

Definitely not a good sign.

When Lucy had done her business, they went back inside, and dread was slowly creeping up his spine. As an act of preservation, he picked the dog up and cradled her to his chest—certain that if Heather was going to do anything to him, she'd reconsider if he was holding the dog.

He was perfectly fine with using the dog as a shield.

And being a coward.

Back in the apartment, all was quiet. Too quiet. He kept Lucy in his arms, and she was licking his chin, perfectly content that she was getting this attention. He walked around a bit and tried to figure out where Heather was and what she was going to do.

Behind him, he heard a noise and turned and saw Heather standing in the doorway to her bedroom. She looked at him, then Lucy, and then back at him, one perfectly arched brow mocking him. "Give me my dog."

He shifted and held Lucy a little more securely against him. "Why?"

"Because I'm asking you to." Her voice was very calm. Eerily so.

"Um, she can just hang with me for a bit. We'll watch some TV."

Heather took a step toward him. "Chris?"

"Yeah?"

"Give me my dog," she repeated.

Crap. Slowly, he crouched down and let Lucy go. He stood up just as slowly. "Look, Heather, about—"

"Where are the Sno-Caps?"

"What?"

"The Sno-Caps. Where are they?"

He reached into his back pocket and pulled the unopened box out and held it out to her. "You want some?"

She took the box from his hands and smiled tightly at him. Chris thought he was out of the woods, that maybe he was making more out of this than there was, when she called his name. He turned and was hit square between the eyes with the box of candy.

"Dammit, Heather! What the hell?"

NINE

Heather couldn't remember ever being so angry with anyone.

In her entire life.

Except maybe Chris himself, when he'd walked out on her dad and the business three years ago.

She wasn't even sure where the anger had come from. It had just been building throughout the evening and culminating her conflicted feelings over the past few weeks. She'd tossed the Sno-Caps, thinking they'd land on the floor and make a satisfying thud.

But the box was heavier than she'd expected, and her aim had been surprisingly good. She blinked in surprise when the box hit Chris in the face.

She'd been furious, but she certainly hadn't intended to hit him in the face.

"What the hell?" he growled again, looking genuinely angry for the first time that evening.

"Sorry," she gasped, still processing her surprise at the accuracy of her aim. "I didn't mean to... I mean, not that you don't deserve it, but—"

He scowled at her. "Why the hell did I deserve that?"

He sounded so sincerely outraged that she suddenly remembered all her righteous indignation. How dare he make himself sound innocent and her sound guilty when he was the one who had always been an ass?

"You know damned well why you deserve it," she snapped. "What were you thinking, sabotaging my date that way?"

"I didn't sabotage your date. I was just being friendly. What the hell?" He muttered out the last words, and he was actually turning away as if he were fed up with her.

As if he hadn't done anything wrong.

Heather didn't know what had gotten into her. She never lost control, and she almost never reacted with anger. She was normally a peacemaker, trying to make sure everyone else was happy. But this was absolutely the last straw with Chris—acting like she was unreasonable and he was completely blameless. It was like some sort of alien force had taken over her body, and there was no way she could stop her hands from clenching into fists at her sides or her mouth from saying what she knew would only make the argument worse. "You were *not* being friendly! Do you really think I'm that stupid? You can act innocent all you want, but I know you did it on purpose."

Chris turned back around with a jerk, his eyes narrowing over obvious resentment. "You're imagining things," he said, slightly more controlled than she was.

"I am not imagining anything. You knew I didn't want me and Dave to hang out with you and Janet, but you maneuvered it anyway. You managed to ruin the whole evening for me, and you did it on purpose."

"Why would I try to ruin the evening for you?"

"I have no idea, but you did! And now you're acting like you didn't do anything. Go ahead and make me sound irrational and melodramatic, just like you did before when I was mad at you for leaving my dad the way you did. But you were wrong then, and you're wrong now, and I'm not just going to put up with it anymore."

That was another thing she hadn't intended to say. Best not to bring up their conflict from the past, since it was a sure way to cause things to unravel between them now. But she'd done it anyway. She just couldn't seem to help it.

His eyes flashed darkly. "So now you're throwing that in my face too? What the hell do you expect from me, anyway?"

"I expect you to be a decent guy. I expect you to care about other people's feelings. One day I'm going to have to learn that's just way too much to expect from you."

"Damn it, Heather. You know that's not fair."

"Not fair? You're the one who pushed his way into my date, just to be an ass."

"I didn't do anything to your date."

"If you didn't do anything, then why is my date going home with another woman?" Heather actually didn't care that much about Dave. She wouldn't have minded at all if this was the only date she ever had with him. She didn't even mind that much that he'd seemed, at the end of the evening, more interested in Janet than in her.

What she minded was that Chris had somehow engineered the disaster of the evening.

"He was just taking Janet home," Chris said, sounding more natural now, as if he'd gotten his own feelings under a tighter rein.

"Yeah, sure he was. Maybe your date was just a prop to you, but Dave wasn't just a prop to me."

Chris immediately snapped back into anger. "What is that supposed to mean? You really think I just use people that way?"

"I don't know. Do you?"

"No! And I didn't realize Dave was the love of your life, or I would have kept Janet away from him."

She made a frustrated sound and reached out to clutch the doorframe to her bedroom, mostly to keep her from lashing out again. "He's not the love of my life! That's not even the point."

"Then what the hell is the point?" Chris had stepped a little closer to her, and he was glaring just as hotly as she was.

"The point is you were acting tonight like a spoiled child or a jealous ex-boyfriend, and I'm not going to put up with it."

He took another step closer to her, so she could almost feel the hot tension radiating off his hard body. "A child?" he asked in a low, rough voice.

She gulped, suddenly hit with the knowledge of how far from a child he was. He was a man. A big handsome masculine man who was suddenly making her think all about sex.

All. About. Sex.

"Or an ex-boyfriend, I said," she managed to reply, hoping she didn't sound as breathless as she felt.

"Oh, you'd know if I was your ex-boyfriend," he murmured, even more thickly than before.

"How?" That wasn't at all what she'd wanted to say, but she couldn't hold back the slightly trembly question.

He moved even closer to her so there were only a few inches between their bodies. "I'd make sure you knew. Although I'm pretty sure I wouldn't be an ex."

She was shaking now and hoping he couldn't see it. "Yes, you would. If I was ever crazy enough to go out with you, it definitely wouldn't last very long. You'd be an ex before you could blink."

"It would never happen."

"Yes, it would. There's no way I would put up with you for long. You might delude yourself into thinking all your arrogance is sexy, but it's mostly just obnoxious." She had no idea why she was saying this. This wasn't at all how the conversation was supposed to have gone.

"But you like it," he said with a hint of a smile.

"I like what?"

He moved even closer. "My arrogance." And then even closer. "And my obnoxiousness."

She was holding herself perfectly still because she was struck with the most powerful desire to touch him. "I do not," she whispered.

"Prove it."

"How?"

"Like this."

Before she knew what was happening, he'd grabbed her head with both his hands and pulled her into a hard, urgent kiss.

Again, it was like that alien force had taken possession of her body, but instead of rage, it was now throbbing with a bone-deep hunger. Her body was out of control again, pressing itself against the hard length of his and clawing at his shoulders as his tongue delved into her mouth with a possessiveness that thrilled her.

Her head spun as Chris slid his hands down to her bottom, cupping her there as he claimed her mouth completely. Then he was lifting her up, and she was wrapping her legs around his waist, and he was carrying her into her bedroom.

Over to her bed.

It was exactly what she wanted. She pulled him down on top of her after he lowered her to the bed, trying to feel his body in every way she could.

Chris seemed to be just as on fire as she was. His body was tight and hard, and his hands and mouth eager and skillful. He climbed over her so he could kiss her again, and she rubbed herself shamelessly against his weight.

She was hot and throbbing all over when he finally raised his head. He raked his eyes over her sprawled body and hot face. "Damn, you drive me crazy, Heather."

"You drive me even crazier," she said, gasping as he began to strip off her clothes, so quickly she was naked before she knew it.

He stared down at her hotly some more, his deeply possessive eyes missing no cleft or curve of her body. "No one could drive a person crazier than you drive me."

"You think that because you've never had to put up with *you*." She gasped again, squirming as he reached out to caress her, his hands stroking from her hips to her breasts.

He was smiling slightly as he leaned back down to take her in another kiss. She responded eagerly, fisting her hands in his hair and rocking her body up into his. She was already so aroused it was almost painful, and she couldn't understand how it was happening.

She'd always liked sex quite well, but it had never, ever been like this.

He kissed her until she could barely breathe, and then he trailed little lines of kisses down her jaw and neck, lingering on her collarbone until she was whimpering, and then finally moving down to her breasts.

And that same alien force somehow had taken possession of her vocal chords too. She couldn't seem to keep quiet as he kissed and fondled her nipples. Her gasps

111

and little moans soon turned into uninhibited cries of helpless need.

She was never this loud, but she couldn't seem to help it as Chris kept teasing her into deeper arousal.

It was clear from his hot, tense body that he was just as turned on as she was, but he didn't appear to be in a hurry. He was still suckling at one breast as his hand finally slipped down lower to feel between her legs.

When he found her clit, she made a loud sound, almost like a sob. And she kept up the helpless sounds as he worked her over with his mouth on her breast and his hand between her thighs.

Then she jerked in surprise when she heard a fierce little growl. Lucy suddenly jumped on the bed beside them, and the little dog started barking viciously at Chris.

Chris turned his head to stare at her. "What's her problem?" he asked hoarsely. His face was slightly flushed, and his eyes were a little dazed, like he'd been just as caught up in the foreplay as she'd been.

Heather made a slight choking sound of amusement as she realized what was wrong with her dog. "She thinks you're hurting me."

Chris stared at the angry little dog for another minute, and then he gave a soft chuckle. "Well, just wait until I really get going and you're screaming your head off. She'll probably attack me."

"Don't flatter yourself. I'm not going to scream my head off."

Without speaking, Chris adjusted his hand so one of his fingers slid inside her, rubbing against her tight inner walls.

She let out a sharp cry of pleasure. Not quite a scream, but close.

Chris chuckled again.

"Shut up," she told him. "That didn't count."

Lucy evidently decided Heather was now both tortured and angry. She growled again and advanced on Chris, her paws making little dents in the comforter. Heather reached out for her. "It's okay," she soothed. "I'm not in trouble. It's okay. You can go lay down."

Lucy looked suspiciously between Heather and Chris, who was still on top of her, but Heather's tone must have mollified her. After another minute, she sniffed at Chris indignantly and then jumped back off the bed to curl up on her cushion in the corner of the room.

Heather was still giggling when she felt a little flicker of knowledge.

What was she doing? Was she really having sex with Chris? What the hell was she thinking?

Before any of these questions could really pierce through the fog of desire in her mind, Chris had kissed her again and she forgot them completely.

They kissed for a minute or two until they'd built back their momentum, and then Chris lowered his mouth to her breast and found her hot arousal with his hand. It felt just as good as it had before, and it wasn't long before she was losing control completely, coming hard all around his fingers as she cried out even louder than before.

She was panting as he raised himself up to kiss her again, and she started to pull off his clothes too.

Soon they were both naked, and Chris had retrieved a condom from his pocket and unwrapped it. She stared at his gorgeous body—hard muscles, smooth lines, dark, coarse hair, hot flesh—as he rolled the condom on and reached over to part her legs.

She wanted this—more than she could remember wanting anything. But she still had no idea why.

"Damn, you're gorgeous," Chris muttered, staring at her body, the way he had earlier, as he pulled her hips into position.

"You're not too bad yourself."

He smiled as he held himself in place and slowly started to enter her, watching her reactions to make sure she was comfortable.

That little gesture—the way his eyes checked out her face—was surprisingly sweet and sensitive, and it made her want him even more.

Both of them were gasping when he'd penetrated her fully and was holding himself above her on straightened arms.

"So good," he was murmuring roughly. "So good." He made a little thrust, like he couldn't hold himself back.

She arched and sucked in a breath at the friction.

"So good," he repeated, rocking into her again. "Wrap your legs around me, baby."

The sound of the words made her clench, and she couldn't help but obey them, raising her legs to wrap them around his hips and hook her feet to keep them in place.

Both of them groaned as the penetration deepened, and then Chris started to thrust for real.

She followed his rhythm, moving her hips with his. He was staring down at her with a strange kind of intensity, and she didn't know what to make of it.

She closed her eyes and tossed her head as the sensations intensified and his motion accelerated.

Everything felt good. So good. But she was still surprised when she felt the momentum of an orgasm tighten inside her after not very long.

"Oh God," she gasped, her eyes flying open and her hands clutching at his shoulders.

"Yes," Chris muttered, still staring down at her face, perspiration starting to bead on his forehead.

"Oh God! Gonna come again." She tightened her legs around him, trying to chase the feeling.

"Yes." His voice was low and thick and possessive. "You're so good. So responsive. Come for me again. I love that you're so eager."

This briefly distracted her. "Eager?" She tried to huff and articulate how wrong this word was, but he was taking her harder and faster now, and it felt so good she couldn't stop herself from babbling. "Oh, God, yes! Make me come. Please, please, Chris, I'm so close!"

His motion had built up until it was almost rough, but it was exactly what she wanted. She clawed her fingernails into his bare back and stifled a scream as the sensations finally peaked.

Chris let out a guttural exclamation as pleasure and release twisted on his face. Then he was letting go completely too, and both of them were gasping and shuddering as their climaxes worked their way through them.

When she'd finally come down from what might have been the best orgasm of her life, she was smiling like a fool.

Chris raised his head so he gazed down at her, stroking her cheek gently. "Definitely eager."

This time, she managed a real huff. "You were pretty eager yourself."

"Guilty as charged."

They smiled at each other, and Heather felt incredibly good all over—body and mind—until Chris pulled out of her at last.

It was only then she started to feel awkward, kind of achy. Naked.

She reached for the covers as Chris got up to take care of the condom and clean himself up some. She didn't know what to say when he came back to the bed.

Fortunately, she didn't have to say anything. He crawled back into the bed with her and took her in his arms, so she felt good again.

So good it wasn't long until she drifted into sleep.

~

Heather slept surprisingly well. She didn't wake up at all until she heard Lucy whining from the floor beside the bed.

Blinking her eyes open, she realized it was morning. Sunlight was starting to stream in from the edges of the blinds, and the clock said it was after six.

Lucy was ready to go outside.

When she rolled over, she realized she wasn't alone in bed. Chris was still beside her, his eyes closed and the covers pushed down to his waist.

He looked softer in sleep—like the hard edges of his body and soul weren't really as hard as they seemed. When she felt her heart melting, she jerked her eyes away from him.

She had been so incredibly stupid.

But she wasn't going to overreact. It wasn't the end of the world. Yes, it had been a mistake. Nothing had changed between them. Chris still could never be a long-term partner.

He would leave her—just as surely as he'd left her father three years ago.

She couldn't let herself be hurt like that.

But she wasn't going to act like this was the end of the world. It was one night of sex. It didn't have to mean anything. Chris would probably be relieved that she wasn't taking it seriously.

When she heard him make a throaty sound, she turned to see he was waking up. He smiled at her as he opened his eyes, looking young and almost sweet.

She couldn't help but smile back, but she soon remembered her resolution and pulled the sheet up to cover her breasts as she sat up.

"Don't hold that sheet up on my account," he said, a smile in his voice.

"We need to get up."

He seemed to wake up a little more and was peering at her face closely. "You're thinking last night was a mistake."

She sighed. "It was. It wasn't the worst mistake in the world, but it was probably kind of stupid. It's just going to complicate things between us."

"Why does it have to?"

"Sex tends to do that." She straightened her shoulders and reminded herself to be mature and reasonable about this. "But I'm sure we can deal with it. We just need to agree it's not going to happen again."

"Why not?"

She blinked. "What do you mean, why not? Because we're never going to be in a relationship, and we don't need things to get messier between us."

"So that's it?" There was no real expression on his face, so she couldn't tell what he was feeling. He didn't look upset or annoyed though, so that was a relief.

"What else is there? We need to work together as business partners. Partners with benefits is totally out of the question."

"That's really what you want?"

She frowned. "Yes. What do you want?" She was suddenly worried that he thought she'd fallen for him and he was trying to be sensitive about it. "We're never going to be in love, and casual sex isn't really my thing. And on top of all that, it's not like you're looking for a commitment or anything permanent."

"Okay." He glanced away from her for a moment, down at Lucy who was still scuttling back and forth on the floor. "Okay."

She had no idea why she felt bad about things, but she did. "Okay. Good." She got out of bed, dragging a throw blanket with her so she wouldn't be naked. She glanced back at him. "It's not that I didn't enjoy last night. You're great and all. It's just that…"

"We can never be in love. Got it."

He sounded basically matter-of-fact, so Heather sighed in relief. "I'm going to take a shower."

"I'll take Lucy out."

Heather stayed in the shower longer than normal, trying to wash away the memory of Chris's hands and lips on her last night, his body above, against, inside her. She should be relieved that they'd dealt with the situation as maturely and painlessly as they had.

But she wasn't.

TEN

We're never going to be in love, and casual sex isn't really my thing.

That chant went on and on in Chris's head all day. Even now, as he was lending a hand hanging drywall, he couldn't think of anything else but Heather's words that morning. More than anything, he wanted to force her to talk to him—to figure out why she felt that way about him. About *them*. But he knew her well enough to know that the harder he pushed, the faster she was going to run.

It's not like you're looking for a commitment or anything permanent.

That was where she was wrong. Not that he'd thought much about it in the past, but now that he was back and was getting to know Heather again, Chris knew what he wanted. He was going to pursue this—of that there was no doubt—but he had to do it carefully.

He just wished he knew how.

How the hell was he supposed to show her that they could be in love and that he *was* looking for something permanent?

With her.

Patience wasn't his strong suit, and his gut was telling him to not let this go. What they had—even before the mind-blowing sex—was worth it. Heather had always had a piece of his heart. When she was younger, he'd always thought she was one of the sweetest girls he'd ever known. Coming back to Preston and seeing the woman she'd become just made her all the more appealing.

By the time five o'clock rolled around, Chris was exhausted and feeling more than a little anxious about going home. Maybe he could go to the office and kill some time there or… damn. Chances were Heather would still be there too. Groaning, he took off his tool belt and walked out to his truck. He tossed his stuff onto the passenger seat and slammed the door, still unsure about what he was going to do.

He drove around aimlessly for a little while. There was no way he could face Heather right now while his mind was still reeling. He knew she had a point about last night—he had purposely sabotaged her date. And he didn't regret it for a minute. Janet was a nice enough woman, but he'd known fairly early on in their date—like the first ten minutes—that she wasn't for him. So when Heather had walked in with her date, it seemed like divine intervention.

Someday, hopefully, she'd see that too.

That still left him no closer to knowing what to do or where to go right now. He was on the outskirts of town when he saw a piece of historical property they had bid on about a week ago. It was a residential building that was vacant, and the town was looking to have it rehabbed. This was the kind of stuff Chris loved the most—the historical homes and properties. The chance to bring something like that back to its original splendor was a major high for him. There was a town truck parked out front, and he decided to pull over and see what was going on.

Climbing out, he was about to call over to see who was walking around when his neighbor Jace Foster appeared around the side of the house.

"Jace!" Chris said, walking over and holding out his hand. "What brings you around here? I thought the town kept you chained to your desk."

Smiling, Jace shook his hand. "Occasionally they let me out to see what's going on."

Chris chuckled. "Glad to hear it. But seriously, what brings you to this site? Is the town ready to make a decision on who they're going to let do the work?"

"That's why I'm here," Jace replied. "I can sit and look at all the proposals at my desk and run numbers—which oddly enough, I love—but on a job like this, where it's a renovation, I needed to see it for myself. All the bids were so different in price that I couldn't wrap my head around it."

"Really? They were that off?"

Jace nodded.

"Any chance of you being willing to tell me where we stand on the short list?"

With a laugh, Jace shook his head. "Believe me, I'm pulling for you. But on a job like this, it will all be presented to a committee for final approval. And it's not a matter of who comes in the cheapest."

"Sometimes that's a red flag in and of itself," Chris quickly said.

"Exactly. We want to make sure that the materials being used are in line with the era of the home, and that everything being done is going to work with what the town is looking for. This particular home—when it's finished—will serve as a museum for Preston. We want everything to be nice, but also be able to stand large crowds and reasonable maintenance."

"All while looking good."

"Yup." Jace looked over his shoulder, toward the house. "Any chance you have time for a quick walk-through with me to answer some questions?"

"Won't that be a conflict of interest? I mean, I could use that time to sway you toward making a decision in my favor."

"Well, shit. I hadn't thought of that."

Sometimes it sucked being honest, but it was something Chris prided himself on. "I'll tell you what. Why don't we go and grab a beer, and should you happen to casually ask a question or two, I'll try to answer it to the best of my ability."

"Sounds good to me," Jace replied. "Flanagans is just around the corner. Want to walk?"

"Sure."

They walked and talked about some general work topics, and Jace only asked a few questions about structural concerns for the house. By the time they grabbed a booth at Flanagans, Chris decided that maybe the key to figuring out what to do with Heather could be found while asking for a little advice from a friend.

"This place is like an institution," Jace said, taking a pull of his beer. "So how are you liking being back in town and living in Preston's Mill?"

"Preston has always been home. And really, living in the building has been great. Tom did a fantastic job on the apartments. Can't ask for a nicer place to live."

Jace nodded. "Hell, yeah. I was lucky to get in when I did. It was like a frenzy when they were being renovated. Everyone wanted in." He took another sip of his beer. "And you're still living there with Heather, right?"

Chris nodded and gave him the abbreviated version of how they ended up living together.

"So it was her dad's idea?"

Nodding, Chris took a drink of his own beer.

"Was he trying to set you two up or something?"

Chris blinked. He'd actually never considered that before. "You know, I have no idea. But I guess it is strange for a dad to arrange something like that for his daughter. Maybe he…" He trailed off, caught up in the new thought.

"And how's it working out for you?" Jace asked, after a moment. "It's gotta be a little bit strange."

Chris hesitated, just enough for Jace to figure out that something was up.

"So are you like… *into* her?"

That made him laugh softly. "You could say that." He paused. "I've always been kind of into Heather. But she was younger, and back before I left town, it seemed like she was too young. But now…"

"Now she's all grown up."

"And things were incredibly awkward in the beginning. She was holding a grudge against me for leaving town and leaving her dad in a lurch, and then… I don't know. It's clear that we're both attracted to each other but she's, um, she's not really…"

"She needs a little convincing? Is that what you're trying to say?"

This had to be the most awkward conversation ever, Chris thought. Guys weren't supposed to talk about this shit, were they?

"Heather thinks that I'm not capable of committing—no doubt she's still holding that grudge because I left town. Not that one has anything to do with the other, but I'm pretty sure she thinks I'm some sort of flight risk."

"And are you?"

Shaking his head, Chris said, "I hope not. I don't think so anymore. Three years ago… hell, I don't know.

Leaving seemed like the thing to do. There was nothing really tying me here to the town—at least, I didn't think so at the time. My mom was my anchor, and even though I was close with Tom, it wasn't the same. I needed... I needed time to just get my head together. It was too hard being here without my mom." He gave a mirthless laugh. "Not exactly the most masculine thing to admit to."

"Your mom was a hell of a woman." Jace began cautiously, "but I seem to remember you taking off a time or two when we were younger."

The memory of some of his teenage antics hit him hard and fast. "Yeah, I know. I never stayed away long."

"No, but you can see where it's been a pattern. So again I ask, are you sure you're staying?"

"I'm here and I'm staying. And I'd like to stay with Heather. I just don't know how to prove that to her."

Jace settled back against the seat and studied him for a minute. "Is she the romantic sort? You know, flowers and candlelight... that kind of crap?"

That had Chris laughing because it was obvious Jace was no better at this stuff than he was. "I have no idea."

"I hate to say it, dude, but you're gonna have to do a little bit of fishing and figure out what her love language is."

"Love language? Did you seriously just say that?"

Jace laughed and looked away. "Trust me. I did."

"You better explain where the hell that came from."

"I saw the book over at Isabella's and decided to check it out."

"Isabella, huh?" Chris asked. "You guys were always tight, even when she used to date Brock back in high school."

Jace just nodded.

"And so you read this book?"

Another nod.

"By any chance, did your reading it have to do with Isabella?"

"Don't ask. Let's just say I've read about it, and it just means you have to figure out what it is that she likes. Is it gifts? Words? Acts?"

"So there's no quick fix to this?"

"Sorry."

Yeah... so was Chris.

He had to figure out Heather's love language. Just great. This might take forever.

~

After that one beer, Chris decided there was no time like the present to get started. He knew Heather really well and had for a long time, but he realized there was a whole lot more that he didn't know about her. But he figured that starting out with the basics couldn't hurt. He texted her and said he was picking up some takeout and asked if she wanted any. When she readily accepted, he took it as a good sign.

Pizza was what he'd been in the mood for, but he figured Chinese would be a little more dignified, and they'd be able to sit at the table and eat together. With the bag of takeout, a small bouquet of wildflowers and a bottle of wine, he was fairly confident that it would look nice without looking like he was trying so hard.

He was striding down the hall and was feeling good when...

"Christopher!"

Dammit. For an old woman, Estelle had bionic hearing.

"Hey, Estelle! No time to talk. Dinner's getting cold!" He held up the bag and tried to keep walking.

"But... but..."

"Have a good night!" he called over his shoulder and quickly opened the door to his apartment and shut it behind him.

"Estelle get you too?" Heather said with a soft laugh. God, she looked beautiful. Her hair was loose, and she was wearing a pair of black yoga pants and a pink tank top. She looked relaxed and just...

Crap, he had it bad.

Lucy danced around his feet, and he had to be careful to avoid stepping on her as he made his way across the room. When he reached the kitchen table, he put everything down and reached down to pet her. "Hey, pretty girl." That seemed to please her, and she quickly pranced away to get some water.

"What's all this?" Heather asked, stepping closer. "What's with the wine and flowers?"

"I was in the mood for a little wine with dinner and the flowers just seemed... I don't know," he shrugged and handed them to her. "They reminded me of you, and I thought you should have them."

Her eyes went wide for a second before she took the flowers and smiled. "I... wow. Thank you." The final word was a breathy sigh as she leaned in and smelled the flowers. "They're beautiful."

Unable to help himself, he reached out and caressed her cheek. "So are you." His voice was gruff as he said it.

"Chris."

He knew she was going to try to tell him that he was wrong or remind him of their conversation from that morning, but he wasn't going to let her. So he quickly diverted her attention. "So I picked up the Chinese food. I grabbed extra dumplings because I remember you saying how much you liked them."

Heather was only mildly flustered by the fast change of subject, and soon they began working together to put the food out. When they sat down, Chris told her about running into Jace and about the property.

"I know my father would love to have his name on that renovation," she said. "He's been eyeing that property for years."

"Jace was pretty tight-lipped about where we stand, but I'm hopeful."

Lucy was back around his ankles. He reached down to pet her and then rose to go and get her something to eat.

"Oh, wait," Heather said as she went to get up. "I'll do that."

"It's not a big deal," he said easily. "Sit and eat. This will only take a second." Then he went about getting Lucy's food and putting fresh water in her bowl. He pet the dog one more time before sitting back down. Heather was looking at him with an odd expression. "What?"

"It's just… I mean… you didn't have to do that. She's my dog, and I don't expect you to—"

"Like I said, it's not a big deal." He smiled at her and was greatly relieved when she smiled back. The rest of the meal passed with great conversation that was largely centered on the business. He loved getting her ideas and found that she had more than just a general working knowledge of what went into the kinds of renovations they did. He had a feeling that if given the chance, Heather probably wouldn't mind getting her hands a little dirty on a job.

He couldn't believe how much his perception of her had changed in only a couple of weeks.

When they were done, they cleaned up together, and before she had the chance, he had Lucy's leash out and was putting it on her.

"Chris, I really don't mind walking her myself," Heather said, coming toward him.

"You look very comfortable and relaxed. You don't want to put shoes back on and go outside, do you?"

"I could throw on some flip-flops—"

"I'm halfway out the door. We'll be back in a few minutes," he said, giving her a quick wave as he opened the door and let Lucy lead the way.

But not before he saw the shy smile on Heather's face.

It wasn't as if he was being cold and calculated about what he was doing. He simply knew that Lucy meant a lot to her, and if he took good care of her dog, it would go a long way in showing how he really was a good guy.

Lucy's tags jingled as they walked, and he silently prayed that Estelle wasn't going to jump out at them again. They made it outside and then back without incident. Once they were back in the apartment, he unhooked the dog and got her a treat. Heather was just coming out of her bedroom and smiled at them.

"Thank you," she said softly. But there was something in her eyes. Something soft and a little dreamy, and he just wanted to dive in and stay right there—keep that look on her face.

"It wasn't a big deal. She's really not such a bad dog." He turned to grab something to drink, but he noticed that Heather was suddenly standing close. And getting closer. "Hi," he said quietly, facing her, and once again he reached up and caressed her cheek.

"Hi."

God, but her voice—that husky whisper—turned him on. He swallowed hard and had to fight the urge to simply haul her in close and kiss her until they were both breathless. It would be beyond satisfying, but he knew it could also work against him. This time she'd need to be the one to make the first move.

And she did.

They were practically touching from head to toe when she looked up at him. "Thank you for dinner."

He smiled down at her, still marveling at how soft her skin was. "My pleasure."

"And the flowers."

This time, he simply nodded.

"And the wine."

She was nervous. He could tell. More than anything, he wanted to tell her that she had nothing to be nervous about. That he wanted her as much as she wanted him, and...

Heather whispered his name as her hand came up and anchored around his nape and pulled his head down to hers. All he could think was, *finally*! The first touch of her lips was soft and tentative. He had to remember to not dive in and devour—no matter how much he wanted to. But it didn't take long for things to spiral out of control, and he wasn't sure who was the one to push it that way.

It was all heat and need as his arms banded around her waist so she was pressed up against him. Heather's hands raked up into his hair and gripped tight. It was all pleasure and a little bit of pain, but more than anything, it was right. His tongue dueled with hers, and for a moment, he considered picking her up and carrying her to bed.

But Heather broke the kiss and took a fast step back. She was breathless and flushed and so damn sexy. He said her name, but that had her taking another step back. "I… I'm sorry. That shouldn't have happened."

What? Seriously? "Yes, it should have," he countered. "Look, I know what you said—"

"This isn't me. I mean this isn't something that I do. Casual," she stammered as she kept making her way back toward her bedroom. "Um, I… I have some work to do. I'll see you in the morning. Good night." And with that, she turned, walked to her room, and quietly shut the door.

He was still trying to catch his breath and figure out what the hell had just happened, when he heard Lucy whimper beside him. When he looked down, she cocked her head to the side and eyed him curiously. "You think you're confused," he said, "join the club."

With nothing left to do, he walked over to the counter, poured himself the rest of the wine and then walked across the room and sat on Flo. The TV was a good distraction, and he pulled up ESPN and settled in for some mindless entertainment. Lucy walked over and tried to jump up in his lap, but it was too far of a jump. Taking pity on her, Chris leaned over, picked her up, and held her in his arms against his chest.

She wasn't the woman he imagined he'd be snuggled up with tonight, but it was obvious she was the only woman willing to take a chance on him.

ELEVEN

Heather got very little sleep. She lay awake in her bed, tossing and turning and brooding about Chris.

It was so hard when you knew you shouldn't do anything, but you wanted to so much.

She wasn't feeling any better or clearer in the morning. Since she was awake, she went into work early and tried to drown her worries with mindless administrative tasks, but it didn't really work. At least Chris didn't put in an appearance all day. Maybe he'd gotten the message at last.

It was bad enough to be attracted to him when he was annoyed with her. It was even worse when he was coming on to her the way he had last night, acting all sweet and romantic.

She wasn't sure how long she'd be able to resist him like that.

Instead of going back to the apartment, she went to see her father after work. He was out of the hospital now and doing pretty well, but she liked to check in on him.

Plus she really didn't want to see Chris.

Her father was lounging in his recliner, watching an old Western, when she knocked on the door and let herself in.

"Hey, Dad," she said with a smile, coming over to kiss him on the cheek so he wouldn't have to get up to greet her. "How are you feeling?"

"Bored."

"The doctor said you needed to take it easy for a week or two."

"I know what he said, but I wasn't cut out for sitting around all day."

"It won't be forever. Try to enjoy it. Do you need something to drink?"

"I wouldn't say no to a beer."

"How about a water? The doctor said you need to drink a lot of it."

Her father grumbled but didn't object, so Heather went to get two bottles of water from the refrigerator. Then she came back to the living room and sat on the couch, feeling tired and confused and kind of glum.

"What's the matter?" her dad asked.

"Nothing really." She tried to smile but didn't really succeed. Her father's kind eyes made her chest hurt, and she found herself saying, "It's just that… that my living situation isn't all that easy."

"It's always hard to live with someone, no matter who it is."

"But it's harder if it's Christopher Dole."

"He's not a bad guy. You know that."

She slanted her father a questioning look, confused by the knowing note in his voice. "He's not all bad—of course he isn't. But that doesn't mean I want to be his roommate. Don't you think there's any way you could rethink this crazy scenario you've set up? We've been doing fine as partners in the business. I don't really think we need to be roommates to make it work out."

She hadn't planned to ask her father for a way out of their deal when she'd come over. That felt kind of weak, and she didn't like to give up on things—no matter how ridiculous those things were. But her chest was fluttering with such anxiety at the thought of more months living with Chris—wanting him the way she did and knowing she couldn't really have him—that she was suddenly desperate.

"Now, Heather," her father said slowly, in that chiding voice he'd always used when she was asking for something unreasonable.

"It's not a silly request, Dad. I did give it a good try. But I don't think you understand how hard it is to live with someone of the opposite sex who you're not... not together with and who you have a complicated relationship with."

"I think I can imagine."

"Can you? I don't know. Most dads wouldn't want their daughters to live with some guy like Chris, especially after what he did to us." She softened her words with an almost teasing look. "You know that, right?"

"I do know that," her father replied with a little smile. "But I'm not most dads, and you're not most daughters." His smile faded as he added soberly, "And what Chris did isn't anything like what your mother did to us."

Heather gulped, the words hitting her like a blow. "What?"

"You heard me."

It took a moment for her to get control of her emotions. To give herself time, she took a long swallow of water. Then she finally said tightly, "They both walked out on us when we trusted them. I don't think it's as different as you claim."

"Of course they're different. *Of course* they are. Chris came back when we needed him."

She couldn't speak over the tightness in her throat, and she had no idea what to say anyway.

Maybe her father was right. Maybe she was holding on to her resentment about his abandonment when it was time to let it go. Maybe the way Chris had returned when her father asked him to was proof that he wasn't who her mother was.

Maybe she was letting her longstanding abandonment issues get in the way of what could possibly be a really good relationship.

"He came back, Heather," her father murmured. "And now he's not going anywhere."

She nodded, trying to rein in a wave of tears. It must be the lack of sleep—making her so emotional. She didn't normally cry this easily.

Her dad must have read her expression because he was silent for a minute until she'd controlled herself and managed to relax again.

Then her father leaned forward. "I know you're trying to protect yourself. And I know you're trying to protect me— the way you always have. But Chris isn't a threat to us, and I think you need to really believe that. So the roommate arrangement still applies."

"Okay," she managed to say. "I'll... I'll think about it."

"Good."

"Do you want me to fix you some dinner?"

"Nah. Glenda Wilson from church brought me over a casserole. I'm just going to heat it up. I need to get out of this chair anyway."

"Okay. I'll... I'll be getting home then." She stood up, suddenly wanting to see Chris, wanting to talk to him.

"Good plan." He had that knowing expression on his face again, and it made Heather rather nervous, in a way she couldn't explain. "I'll talk to you tomorrow."

As she made her way down the front walk, she paused in front of the little birdhouse that hung in the tree, emotion catching suddenly in her throat as she stared at it.

Her mother hadn't come back—even when she and her father had needed her. She hadn't been there when Heather had her first period, when she'd started to date, when she was trying to decide where to go to college.

Her mother wasn't here now, when it felt like she might be starting to fall in love.

But Chris had come back. Her father was right. It was entirely different with Chris.

She wasn't going to let her old fears and insecurities keep her from something really good.

She nodded at the birdhouse, feeling a surge of determination again.

She was going to talk to Chris.

~

When Heather returned to Preston's Mill, she was so fluttery she was having trouble breathing. It felt like something important was about to happen, but she wasn't even sure what it was.

She tried to stay quiet as she walked down the hall, but she must not have been quiet enough. Estelle poked her head out the door just as Heather was passing.

"What's going on, young lady?" Estelle demanded, her hair wound tightly in her standard pink sponge curlers.

Heather jerked to a stop. "Good evening, Mrs. Berry," she managed to say with her normal politeness. "What do you mean?"

"Something is going on. I've been feeling vibes. Your young man has been stalking around for a couple of days like a bear who's lost its honey, and you look as jumpy as a rabbit who wants to get a carrot but is too nervous to cross the fence."

Heather didn't actually appreciate being referred to as a rabbit, but she had to admit that Estelle had picked up on the vibes correctly. The woman might be wacky, but she was also strangely insightful. "It's... nothing to worry about," she said at last, having no idea what else to say.

"I'm not worried," Estelle said with a scowl. "I'm tired of all this tension in the air. Figure it out with your young man, would you? I'm old and I need peace."

Then the old lady slammed the door in Heather's face.

Heather stared for a moment, not sure whether to laugh or blush or be annoyed.

She ended up doing none of those things. She just kept walking toward her own apartment door.

When she entered, Chris was in the kitchen, loading some groceries into the refrigerator. He glanced back as she stepped inside. "What was that?" he asked. "It sounded like a door slammed."

"It was Estelle. She was..." Heather trailed off, shrugging. "She was being Estelle."

"She gave me a little lecture when I came in," Chris said, turning around and leaning against the granite counter. "She told me she was too old to put up with vibes, and I was to stop emitting them immediately."

Heather giggled, leaning down to greet an ecstatic Lucy. "She told me the same thing."

Suddenly feeling better about everything, she put down her purse, scooped up Lucy, and walked into the kitchen area to join Chris.

Chris's eyes were soft on her face, as if he recognized her altered mood. "So I guess we need to stop emitting vibes," he murmured.

"Yeah." She cuddled Lucy, partly because she wanted to and partly because it gave her something to do with her hands. "I guess we need to work on that."

"How do you suppose we do that?" He stepped closer to her, looking handsome and sexy and fond and irresistible.

"I... I don't know."

"Don't you?"

Heather swallowed. "I, uh, actually I've been thinking."

"About what?" His expression changed slightly, tightening with something that looked like hope.

"About... us. My dad says I've been holding on to a grudge against you for no good reason, and I'm wondering if he's right."

Chris took a moment to process this, and then his gaze grew even softer. He lifted a hand to stroke her cheek with his knuckles. "And is he right?"

Heather swayed toward him, trying to make her mind work with any degree of coherence. "I think maybe he is. It's... it's hard for me to trust. I have a few issues with people leaving me after what happened with my mom."

"That's totally understandable. And I know I did walk out on you and your dad when you both trusted me. I'm not going to do it again."

"I hope not." She swallowed hard again, suddenly terrified by what she seemed to be saying. "I'm not saying that I'm all in or anything. It's still early for us. But I do think we're good together, and I'm willing to give it a try."

His hand grew still, cupping her cheek. "When you say give it a try, do you mean…"

"Us. Like this. I'm willing to give it a try."

He gave a little groan and pulled her into a kiss. It was warm and urgent and emotional, and Heather was lost in it almost immediately. She wrapped one arm around his neck, still holding Lucy in the other—and opened her mouth to the advance of his tongue.

She wasn't sure how far the kiss would have gone had Lucy not decided that something very strange was happening. The dog stretched up and gave Chris's jaw a hard jab with her muzzle, the way she did when she was checking out a possible threat.

Chris broke off the kiss with a huff.

Heather giggled and leaned over to set Lucy down, giving her a few reassuring strokes. "It's okay, Miss Lucy," she murmured. "He's not doing anything wrong."

Chris reached down to pull Heather to her feet. "I sure hope not. But maybe I could use some more practice."

Heather smiled at him, washed with excitement and pleasure and something akin to hope. "More practice will have to wait. Lucy needs to go out, and I'm kind of hungry."

"What about if I take you out for dinner?"

Heather's eyes widened. "Like a date?"

"Yes, like a date. I thought that's what you meant when you said you'd give it a try."

"It is what I meant," Heather admitted, nervousness mingling with all her other emotions. "And I'd like to go out with you."

She was also kind of scared though. If they went out, then everyone in town would know.

And that would make this thing between them real.

~

Chris took her to eat at one of the nicer restaurants in town. Nothing in Preston was particularly fancy, but this restaurant had good food and a pleasant, quiet ambience, and it wasn't very crowded on a weekday evening.

Chris was charming the whole time, and she could tell he was making an effort to show her what a good date he could be. It was almost exhilarating, the knowledge that he wanted her so much that it was important to him that she continue to go out with him. He told her funny stories, gave her subtle, thoughtful compliments, and gazed deeply into her eyes. His smile was making her giddy, and his warm laughter was making her melt.

By the time they'd ordered dessert, Heather was well on her way to being swept off her feet. She'd had two glasses of wine, but she'd been afraid to drink any more for fear her inhibitions would be lowered so much she'd do something stupid.

She was going to give this a try. It was obviously what both she and Chris wanted, and her father was right about her not holding on to her resentment when Chris didn't deserve that.

But she also didn't want to jump headlong into a relationship that might end up hurting her.

As she'd expected, they saw several people they knew, and Heather tried to ignore all the interested looks from people who hadn't expected her and Chris to be dating.

That was the problem with a small town. One date could suddenly blow up into a full-fledged relationship in the town's eyes.

As they were leaving the restaurant, Chris asked, "Do you want to walk a little? It's a nice night."

"Sure." She smiled as he took her hand, and they started down the main street of Preston. It was dark out now, but the town had done a good job with street lights, and there were several other people out, walking to their cars or just taking a stroll down to the river.

"Chris! Heather!" The voice called out from the opposite side of the street, and Heather turned to see Jace and an attractive brunette getting into the town truck that Jace drove.

Heather recognized Isabella, whom she remembered from high school, and she waved over at both of them.

Jace and Isabella seemed to be going somewhere, so they didn't stop to chat. When they'd driven off, Heather said, "They seem to hang out a lot for people who aren't dating."

"I'm thinking that Jace wants to change that."

"I don't think Isabella has ever thought about him as anything but a friend."

"Yeah. That makes it kind of awkward for Jace, doesn't it?" Chris seemed more amused than sympathetic.

"You shouldn't laugh at someone else's romantic woes," Heather chided, smiling up at him rather sappily. Her excitement had definitely outpaced her nervousness, and she couldn't look away from his familiar face.

"Yeah, but my romantic woes seem to have taken a definite upward swing." They'd reached the side of the river, where the town had built a cute little boardwalk. Chris reached out and put his hands on her hips to pull her closer to him.

"Remember we're taking this slow." She said that mostly because she thought she should. She didn't want to take it slow at all. She wanted him to kiss her, touch her, make love to her. She never wanted him to stop.

"I remember," he murmured. He leaned down and spoke in a thick, enticing voice against her ear. "I can go as slow as you want."

Her breath hitched, and her hands moved of their own accord, pressing eagerly against his chest and holding on to his shirt.

He was smiling as he leaned into her. "Is this too fast?"

"No," she admitted. "This is just right."

He kissed her, and her nerves and her lingering fears of abandonment were completely forgotten.

TWELVE

The last time they'd made love, it had been wild and frantic.

This time, Chris wanted slow. He wanted to touch and learn and savor every inch of Heather. And as far as he was concerned, sleep was highly overrated. They had all night.

And it looked like part of it was going to be spent trying to get home with a raging hard-on.

As much as he hated to, he ended the kiss. Resting his forehead against hers, Chris took a minute to catch his breath. "I know the walk here seemed like a good thing, but right now, all I can think about is…"

"The long walk home?" she said with a soft laugh.

"Do you think anyone would notice if we just ran across town?"

"This is what happens when we laugh at someone else's romantic woes. Remember that."

Chris laughed and then reached down and took one of her hands in his. "Come on. Let's go home."

Home. He hadn't allowed himself to think about having one of those in over three years, and right now it just seemed to fit perfectly. The apartment with Heather—while not perfect—was a home in every sense of the word.

And if they didn't get there soon, he was pretty sure they'd get arrested for doing something indecent in public. Behind him, Heather giggled as he walked briskly—no doubt reading his mind. He wanted to comment on it, but that would mean wasting time.

By the time they reached his truck, he was a little out of breath. When they climbed in, rather than starting the engine, he leaned in and kissed her again. And even though he swore he'd go slow, it didn't seem to be what either of them wanted right now. It was deep and erotic and oh-so-wet. The feel of her tongue teasing his nearly had him pulling her into his lap and making good on the thought of them being indecent in public.

"Chris?" she murmured against his lips.

"Yeah?"

"Drive," she said, even as her nails were raking against his scalp and leaning in for another kiss.

"Baby," he growled softly, "I'm gonna need to keep my eyes on the road for that."

"Well, damn."

He knew exactly how she felt.

Clearing his throat, Chris pulled back, quickly got situated, and pulled out of the parking lot. They drove in silence, even as he was mentally cursing every red light and stop sign. Ten minutes later, they pulled up to Preston's Mill, and as soon as the truck was in park, they were quickly climbing out.

At the front of the truck, Chris took Heather's hand and pulled her with him up to the building, inside, and up the stairs. Their door was in sight, and he was fumbling with his keys when…

"There you two are!" Estelle said, stepping out into the hallway. "I was wondering…"

"Not now, Estelle!" they yelled in unison as they all but ran the last ten feet to their door. Chris hastily unlocked it, and as soon as they were through the door, he slammed it shut and reached for Heather. She instantly stepped into his

143

arms, and this kiss was just as hot and carnal as the one in the truck minutes ago.

And then Chris remembered... slow.

Clearly, that was going to be difficult for both of them because it didn't take much for them each to lose control. And as much as he hated to—again—he broke the kiss and gave her a lopsided grin. "We said slow."

Heather nodded, licking her lips slowly. "I know."

"That wasn't feeling slow."

She shook her head. "Nope."

He was about to make another comment, when Lucy started barking at the two of them. Chris knew the right thing to do—the gentlemanly thing to do—was to offer to take the dog out, but he needed a moment.

"Why don't you take her out," he suggested, "and I'll... I'll pour us some wine."

Heather smiled. "I'll be back in five minutes." Then she gave him a quick kiss on the lips and reached down to scoop up Lucy.

While she was gone, Chris did pour them each a glass of wine and then carried them to his bedroom. He thought about putting them in Heather's room, but he had the bigger bed, and in order for him to do all the things he wanted to tonight, he wanted the space to spread out.

He took a minute to straighten up the space, pull down the blankets and turning off lights, leaving only one small bedside lamp on. Looking around, he suddenly felt nervous. Everything looked neat. Clean. He wished he had some candles. Then he thought about setting up his iPhone and playing some music but didn't think there was time to figure that all out. Then he shook his head with disbelief. This was probably the first time he'd ever even remotely tried to set the scene for seduction.

And really, it seemed crazy since they were both clearly already seduced.

"Nice room," Heather said from the doorway, and Chris turned in surprise. He'd never heard her come back in.

He grinned and shrugged. "Thanks."

She walked toward him until they were toe to toe. They simply stared at one another for a long moment—Chris's hands on her waist, her arms looped around his shoulders. "Hi."

"Hi."

This time when he bent to kiss her, it was slow. The kiss was soft. Gentle. Almost chaste. His hands began to skim up her ribcage, taking her top with them. Lazily, Heather raised her arms over her head and let him take the garment off. She stood before him in white lace, and it looked magnificent.

After looking his fill, he lifted his hands to her breasts and gently caressed them, kneaded them, until she was panting. Her head lolled back, her lips parted, and she looked so damn sexy that he needed to think about lumber inventory for a minute to get himself back in check.

They moved together as if their steps were choreographed—turning together as the rest of their clothes fell away. Chris gently guided her down to the bed and covered her body with his. They both sighed at the skin-on-skin contact.

He kissed her lips, her cheek, her throat.

He gently fondled her breasts before letting his mouth replace his hands there.

And as he teased and laved at her nipple, his hand slid down—memorizing her curves as he made his way down and honed in on where she was hot and wet. For him. He growled with approval at the same time Heather sighed his name.

It was all the talking either of them did this time. Like him, she seemed content to let her hands explore him this time, and rather than speaking, they simply enjoyed the sensation of just feeling.

And she felt so damn good.

Sliding one finger, and then two, into her as she slowly pumped her hips was perfect. The way her back arched to press her breast more securely against his lips was beyond sexy. And when he heard the catch in her breath, right before she came for him, it was the most erotic sound he'd ever heard.

He covered her lips with his quickly, right before he reached over to his nightstand for a condom. Leaning back, he looked down at her sprawled naked across the bed. All he could think of was how perfect she looked there and how this was where he wanted her to be, always.

"Chris," she whispered, a plea. "Please."

With the condom on, he came down slowly on top of her again, relishing how her legs wrapped around him. Heather's hands raked up his back and into his hair again to pull him down for another kiss as he slid into her.

In and out. In and out. Slowly. Each entry was ecstasy, while every retreat was almost more than he could bear. Her hips raised to meet his, and he nuzzled her neck. "Let me love you," he whispered. "Just let me love you."

"Yes," she sighed.

Unable to help himself, he quickened the pace—had to. It was almost beyond his control. Heather met him thrust for thrust. Her legs tightened around his waist, and Chris pulled back and met her gaze, loving the look on her face as she came.

And only then did he allow himself to go over the edge, crying out her name as he did.

For long moments, neither spoke. They each took that time to catch their breath. Chris rolled to the side, pulling Heather in close beside him. Her hand rested over his still rapidly beating heart, and he held it there.

There was a small noise next to the bed, and he looked over to see Lucy sitting there staring at them.

"We're really going to have to do something about her," he said softly. "I don't think I like having an audience every time we make love."

Heather chuckled softly. "I'll have a talk with her tomorrow."

Chris kissed her on her forehead. "Maybe you should do it tonight."

She yawned. "Tonight? Why?"

"Because I'm not quite done exploring you yet."

Heather's eyes went wide, right before his words sank in. Then she gave him a sexy grin and said, "Lucy, we have to talk!"

~

Two weeks later, Chris walked in the door after work and smiled. Heather was in the kitchen feeding Lucy, and something was cooking on the stove. She turned when she heard the door close. "Hey!" she said with a smile.

He walked right over to her and kissed her soundly. "Sorry I'm late."

"It's fine. I stopped to do some grocery shopping on the way home, so I just got in a few minutes ago myself."

"Something smells good. What are you making?"

Walking over to the stove, she gave the skillet a quick shake. "It's a Chinese stir-fry with shrimp and scallops. I've got some rice going too."

"Sounds good." He walked over to the refrigerator, grabbed a beer, and looked around to see if she was drinking anything yet. When he spotted her glass of wine, he knew she was good. "You know, you still have never made me any cookies."

She looked surprised. "Why would I?"

"I don't know. You make them for everyone else. I'm a big fan of cookies, you know."

She laughed, her expression fond. "I'll keep that in mind."

"I saw your dad's car at the office today. I was going from the Martin job to the Lawson one and didn't have time to stop in. Is he doing okay?"

For the next few minutes, she talked about her father and his health while she continued to cook. Chris set the table and then played with Lucy for a bit. This was their routine now, and even though it was far more domesticated than anything he had ever imagined for himself, he was loving every minute of it.

"I'm going to take her out while you finish cooking," he said.

"Thanks."

As was their habit, he and Lucy made their way downstairs and out the front door where she wandered the yard and did her business quickly. By the time they were back up in the apartment, Heather had their dinner on the table. Chris gave Lucy a treat to keep her busy while they ate.

"So I was thinking," Heather said as they sat down, "Dad is really feeling a little left out of the loop because of his recovery. What if we had him over for dinner one night?"

That surprised Chris. Not that he didn't want Tom to come over, but they hadn't talked about how they would handle things in front of him. "And you're comfortable with that? With him being here... with us?"

She looked at him oddly. "Of course. Why wouldn't I?"

"I just thought that since we... I don't know... I guess I wasn't sure you were comfortable with him knowing about us."

Then she gave him a patient smile. "I'm not ashamed of us, Chris. And I'm not trying to hide it. I know we've been busy at the office, and you've got a lot of job sites to manage right now, so we haven't exactly been out on the town but—"

"I'm not ashamed or trying to hide us either," he said quickly. "I just don't want to shock Tom or freak him out. I mean this was all his idea—us living together—but I'm not sure whether he's prepared for what it... led to."

"Us being lovers?" She wasn't angry. If anything, she was smirking at him.

"I was going to say that he didn't think it would lead to us being boyfriend and girlfriend," he countered.

"Boyfriend and girlfriend? What are we, in high school?" she teased.

Okay, she had a point. That did sound a little ridiculous. "How about we just say we're together? Lovers is going to have people thinking thoughts that I don't want people imagining about us."

"Naked thoughts?" she said with a laugh.

"Exactly! And the only one who is allowed to think of you naked is me."

"Right back at ya."

"Good. As long as we're clear on that." Then he turned and looked at Lucy and shook his fork at her. "And that goes for you too. If you don't quit sneaking in the room or scratching at the door, I'm going to get you a kennel and keep you in there!"

"She said she was sorry," Heather said, unable to hide her amusement. "And that accident she had in your shoe? Well, that was more upsetting for her than it was for you."

"Was it upsetting for her?" he mocked playfully. "Because I was the one with poop on my foot, not her."

"And the whole incident with Flo…"

Chris held up a hand to stop her. "Just… don't. It's still too hard to talk about it."

Heather rolled her eyes. "It's just a small tear! I told you I'd fix it."

"It's not the tear that hurt but the intent." He glared over at Lucy. "She's pissed at me, and she went right for the jugular."

"It's just a chair."

He gasped dramatically. "And my foot. Let's not forget about that, shall we?"

And then they both burst out laughing. And yeah, he really was kind of annoyed that in this whole great new phase of life Lucy was seriously messing around with him, but he hoped she'd get over it. Sooner rather than later. Who knew a dog could be so spiteful?

"Maybe the two of you can watch some TV together after dinner. I'd really love to take a nice bubble bath. It's been ages since I've soaked in that wonderful tub."

Chris remembered the last time she'd done it. "And I'm supposed to settle for snuggling with killer over there while I know you're naked and covered in bubbles only a few feet away? How is that fair?"

"How about this? I take my bubble bath, you and Lucy make nice and watch some TV, and when I'm done, you can help me dry off?"

He considered his options. "I kind of prefer making you wet," he teased, waggling his eyebrows.

"I'm totally on board with that too."

THIRTEEN

The following Wednesday, Heather was sitting at the desk in her office, trying to clear out some email but mostly wondering what Chris and her father were talking about.

Her father had finally been allowed to come back to the office for a few hours a day this week, and she'd been vigilant about his not overdoing it. It was almost time for him to leave for the day, but Chris had gone in to say hello twenty minutes ago, and he was still in there talking to her dad.

With the office door closed.

She attempted to push her curiosity away and focus on the words on the computer screen, but she wasn't particularly successful.

What the hell were they talking about in there for so long? And why had Chris closed the door? If they were talking about the business, then she had a right to hear what was said. And if they were talking about something personal, then what on earth could it be?

She knew she was more sensitive to private conversations than she should have been because of her parents' tense conversations in their bedroom before her mother walked out. So she breathed deeply and told herself to get a grip.

She loved and trusted her father. She cared about Chris… a lot. They weren't in there talking about anything that was going to hurt her. She wasn't going to let her insecurities from the past affect her happiness right now.

And she was happy. She was doing the work she'd always wanted to do. Her father was getting a lot better.

And she had Chris. Something she'd never even knew she wanted.

She pretended to work for another ten minutes until her father's office door finally swung open and Chris appeared, his back facing out as he said a few last words to her dad.

"Sounds good, then," Chris said. "We'll talk later."

Heather fought another swell of curiosity and smiled as Chris turned in her direction. He grinned and walked into her office.

"Hello," she said, turning her chair away from the computer. "That was a long conversation."

"Yeah." He was grinning at her, and he didn't appear to notice that her comment had invited him to explain the subject of their long conversation. He walked around her desk so he could lean down and kiss her lightly on the lips. "I've been waiting all day to do that."

She experienced an immediate wash of pleasure at the words and gesture, but it was tempered by lingering questions and a good dose of common sense. "Yeah, right." She quirked her lips up to show she was teasing. "I bet you haven't thought about kissing me all day."

"You'd definitely lose that bet." His voice was warm and textured in that way she really liked. She couldn't believe she was dating him. She couldn't believe it was going so well.

She wasn't going to act like some sort of jealous, insecure child and demand he tell her what he was talking to her father about. "So what were you and Dad talking about for so long?"

Chris's expression changed. For a moment, he looked almost trapped, but it was gone before she could fully recognize it. He gave her a casual smile. "Nothing. Just a couple of jobs that are giving me trouble."

"What jobs are giving you trouble?" Her eyes widened since she was genuinely surprised to hear anything of the kind. Chris seemed to have everything totally under control. He was going to be as good at this work as her father was.

"It's no big deal." He shrugged, clearly trying to brush off the topic. "So what did you have in mind for dinner tonight?"

"Chris," she said frowning, "is something going on? If it involves the business, then I need to know what it is."

"It's nothing. It's not really about the business. We're not trying to wrest control away from you, you know."

"I know that. I'd never think anything like that. I was just wondering what you were talking about, and you won't tell me."

He was starting to look a little impatient. "It's nothing, Heather. Don't nag."

She sucked in a breath. He couldn't have said anything else that would have made her shut up more quickly if he'd been trying. She didn't ask again, but she was left feeling confused and anxious.

Chris and her father shouldn't have any secrets from her, but if they didn't, then why wouldn't Chris tell her what was going on?

She didn't like secrets. She didn't like private conversations. She knew all too well the heartbreak they could lead to.

~

She was still stewing about it that evening, even as she kept giving herself mental lectures about not blowing something little out of proportion.

Both of them stayed at work later than normal, so they just made soup for dinner, and they ate as they watched television after they got home. On the surface, everything seemed perfectly fine between them, but Heather couldn't help but wonder why he wouldn't just tell her what he'd been talking about to her father.

She'd gone over every possibility in her mind, and nothing she could possibly think of would demand to be kept secret—not from her, anyway.

Chris came into her room at bedtime, but she was too unsettled to have sex. He pulled her into his arms and held her in the dark, and she felt a little better.

He was a good guy. He was into this relationship as much as she was. Whatever was going on couldn't be bad.

"What's the matter, baby?" he murmured, evidently feeling some kind of tension in her body.

"Nothing. Not really. I mean it's nothing big."

"But it's something. What is it? You've been quiet all evening."

She cleared her throat, determined to be mature and honest about her feelings, since this relationship felt like it might be for real. "It's just... You know, before my mom left us, when I was a girl, she and my dad had all kinds of secrets and private conversations. They... they still make me kind of nervous."

"I can understand that. It's hard to shake feelings like that."

Since he sounded sincere—and very sweet—she found the courage to ask, "Anyway, I just mention it because secrets still make me... unreasonably anxious. And I'm still wondering what you and Dad were talking about this afternoon in his office. And I'm wondering why you wouldn't tell me."

"Oh." He paused, and it felt to Heather like he was searching for the right thing to say. "It was nothing, Heather. Nothing for you to be anxious about. Just work stuff."

"If it was work stuff, then why can't you tell me what it is?"

"I can't even really remember. I get that you still have some issues from your mom, but you're not actually going to make a big deal about something so silly, are you?"

His question effectively silenced her. She didn't want to have issues. She didn't want to be silly. She wanted to do the right thing, and maybe that meant swallowing over her mental discomfort and the lingering sick feeling in her gut. "Okay," she managed to say. "Sorry to make a big deal about nothing."

"It really is nothing," Chris murmured, brushing a few kisses into her hair. "You know I'd never do anything to hurt you. And your dad would die before he let something like that happen to you."

"I know."

"So there's nothing to worry about, right?"

He was trying to make her feel better. It was nice.

But she would rather have had the truth.

"Right," she said, feeling trapped between her urgent questions and a resistance to behaving unreasonably.

Sometimes it was really hard to be a reasonable adult.

"If you need some way to channel any of that anxiety, I can think of something we might do," he drawled.

She smiled, rolling over to face him. "Can you?"

156

"Oh, yeah."

She hadn't really been in the mood, but he looked so adorably rumpled and sexy—and he was trying so hard to make her happy—that she changed her mind.

So they ended up having sex after all.

~

The following day, Chris had to work late at a job site, so Heather went to visit her father after work.

She liked to stop by at least a couple of days a week so she could pick up a little and make sure he had groceries in the refrigerator. He was sitting in his recliner, as usual, watching the evening news rather drowsily, but he perked up immediately when he saw she'd stopped at the Italian restaurant in town and brought in takeout.

"Thanks," he said, sticking a finger into his pasta to see how hot it was and then immediately digging in. "I'm starving."

She chuckled and opened a bottle of beer before handing it to him. "You've got a fridge full of food."

"Yeah, but all of it is healthy. I wanted something good."

She opened her takeout container and sat on the couch near him to eat. "So you've been feeling all right today?"

"Yeah," he mumbled, his mouth full.

"You did some exercise?"

He rolled his eyes. After he swallowed, he said, "I walked around the neighborhood. I'm doing fine, Heather."

Her chest tightened slightly, remembering how scared she'd been when he was taken to the hospital. She might want him to live forever, but that wasn't going to happen. One day, she would lose him.

One day, she'd be all that was left of her family.

"Don't get all morbid on me," he grumbled.

"I didn't say anything."

"I could see morbidity on your face."

She chuckled. "I'm not being morbid. I promise."

"Good." He paused while he took another bite. "How's Chris?"

"He's fine." She felt slightly uncomfortable because of her worries from yesterday, and she didn't meet her father's eyes.

This was evidently all the clues he needed to pick up that something was wrong. "He's treating you right, isn't he?"

"Yeah. Yes, of course he is." She smiled, trying to clear her face. She'd never been any good at hiding her feelings—especially from her father. "He's a good guy."

"I think this time he's going to stick around, you know."

She nodded. "I hope so."

"You're still not sure? I thought you two were all lovey-dovey now."

She giggled at his choice of words. "We're... we're doing good. But we haven't been together very long. You don't make commitments that soon."

"I don't know why not," her father said, his forehead wrinkling. "In my day, we didn't dilly-dally around, like you kids seem to do."

"Yeah, but it's different now. And I'm not going to jump into something without knowing for sure it's going to work out."

He frowned again, differently this time. "You never know for sure if it's going to work out."

There was a bittersweet edge to his tone, and she knew immediately he was thinking about her mother. When he'd fallen in love with her, when they'd gotten engaged and then married, he must have genuinely believed it would last forever.

He couldn't have known she would walk out on him ten years later and never look back.

The thought made Heather's throat hurt, and her eyes blurred over slightly. She still didn't understand how her mom could have done that to her father, to *her*, but it happened in this world—every day.

The day might come when Chris would walk out on her.

She was suddenly terrified, realizing how much she'd already invested emotionally in this relationship. They may have just been together for a few weeks, but she would be utterly crushed if he left her.

"Now you're stewing again," her father said, looking like his normal self again as he focused on another forkful. "If you're not willing to take a risk, you'll never get to experience love."

"I know." She swallowed hard. "I know that. It just seems smart to be careful until it really seems like the right... the right person. A person who's really going to be open and honest with you, who will share their whole life with you."

"No argument here."

She sighed and leaned back against the couch. Then she asked before she could stop herself. "What were you and Chris talking about in the office yesterday?"

She didn't want to be a person who would obsess over something so trivial, but evidently she was.

Her dad blinked. "What? Oh, nothing. Just some work stuff."

"What work stuff? If it's important, then I should know."

"It wasn't important. I can't even remember what job it was about."

He was brushing it off, exactly as Chris had. Maybe she was ridiculous to be making a big deal about it, but both his response and Chris's had seemed a little fake to her.

Something was going on. And neither one of them was telling her what it was.

For just a moment, she felt exactly as she had at eight years old, staring at her parents' closed bedroom door, knowing something terrible was happening behind it but not having any way of finding out what it was.

With a sigh, she let the subject drop and finished her meal, but she got up twenty minutes later feeling even more worried and depressed than she had been earlier.

Her father used to tell her everything. She had no idea why he wasn't telling her now—and why he was telling Chris instead.

She was throwing their trash away and cleaning up the kitchen a little when she noticed the bottom drawer in the hutch was hanging open. She went to close it and saw that it was mostly empty.

She knew her dad kept a lot of papers and files in the drawer, so she blinked down at the drawer. "Have you been doing some purging?" she asked loudly enough for him to hear in the other room.

"No. What do you mean?" he called out.

"This bottom drawer of the hutch." She stuck her head back into the living room to talk to him. "It's empty. What happened to all the papers?"

"Oh." He looked startled for a minute. "I gave some stuff to Chris to look over."

"If they were work related, they should have gone to me."

"I know. They weren't work related. They're just some ideas I had for... for projects and such that I wanted him to review and give me his opinion on. I wanted his expertise."

She relaxed. That made sense. She wouldn't be any good at giving her father expert advice on projects. And it was fine if he wanted to get Chris's opinions. She needed to stop overreacting. Just because something felt off, strange, hidden, didn't mean that it actually was.

"All right," she said with a smile. "Do you want some dessert? I can make you some mixed fruit or something."

Her father made a face. "You don't have any ice cream to put it on, do you?"

~

Heather was feeling a little better when she returned to their apartment in Preston's Mill an hour later.

Everything was going fine with Chris, and she and her father were still close. Nothing had changed. She wasn't going to let her lingering issues with her mother ruin her life now that things were going really well.

Chris's truck wasn't in the parking lot when she arrived, so he must have still been working. It was seven thirty now. Surely he'd be finished up at the job soon.

She was walking down the hall when Estelle stuck her head out of her apartment. "Good evening, young lady. What's all the commotion?"

Heather blinked. "What commotion?" The hall was completely quiet, and there was no one else in sight.

"I heard commotion earlier. People hurrying up and down the hallway."

"Oh. I don't know. I just got here." Heather waved, about to continue to her place when she noticed her apartment door was hanging open. She stopped abruptly.

"Why is your door open?" Estelle demanded, stepping out of her apartment wearing a long red flannel nightgown and her normal pink curlers.

"I have no idea. Maybe Chris left…" She trailed off. Chris wasn't even here.

"Young lady, don't you dare enter that apartment alone. There might be thieves and rapists waiting for you."

Torn between amusement and genuine nerves, Heather gave a little giggle. "I'm sure it's nothing." Then she raised her voice to call, "Chris? Are you in there?"

There was no answer.

Estelle shook her head. "Wait here. I'll be right back."

Heather had no idea what the old lady was going to do until she returned carrying a baseball bat and a golf club.

She handed Heather the golf club. "Now we can go investigate."

Choking slightly in response, Heather accepted the club and walked with Estelle down the hall toward her apartment. Or rather, she walked and Estelle kind of stalked her way down, brandishing her bat, as if she were on the hunt for prey.

"Hello!" Heather called out when they'd gotten to the opened doorway. "Is anyone here? Chris?"

When nothing but silence greeted them, they walked inside. Heather almost tripped on a cardboard box that was set down in the floor of the entryway.

Before they could get any farther inside, there was a sound from behind them.

Both of them whirled around, and Estelle swung her bat.

Chris managed to catch the bat before it clobbered him. "What's going on?" he demanded gruffly.

"Oh, dear," Estelle gasped. "I'm so sorry, dear boy. I thought you were a criminal."

"Well, I'm not." Chris's eyes moved over to Heather, who had lowered her golf club. "Everything all right?"

"The door was opened, and you didn't seem to be here, so we were just being safe," Heather explained, a little embarrassed, although they'd been perfectly right to be careful, given the situation. "Where have you been? I didn't see your truck."

"Yeah. Uh…" He trailed off, the strangest expression on his face.

Then suddenly, Heather remembered something. "Where's Lucy?"

Chris was just opening his mouth to reply when another voice sounded from farther down the hall. "I found her! I found her!"

Heather stepped past Chris and looked down the hall to see Jace striding toward them with Lucy in his arms.

Making a little sound in her throat, Heather reached out to take her dog as Jace came near. "What on earth happened?" she exclaimed.

"I'm sorry," Chris said, rather thickly. "I was carrying in a couple of boxes and left the door opened too long. She got out, and then I couldn't find her. I even drove around the block just now, looking for her. Where was she?" That last question was directed toward Jace.

"Down in the laundry room," he explained, sweating slightly, like he'd been hurrying around, searching for the dog. "She was making up to old Mr. Robinson."

Heather's mind was a tumble, but she managed to work out that there had been a panic about possibly losing her dog but the danger was over now. She cuddled Lucy close to her. "She doesn't usually run away," she said. "But sometimes she likes to explore."

A few minutes later, they'd properly thanked both Jace and Estelle for their help, and she and Chris were alone in the apartment. She was still cuddling Lucy as she glanced down at the box in the entry hall, which was evidently the reason for the door to have been left open.

"Are you mad?" Chris asked, still looking hot and hassled. He must have been really nervous about losing Lucy.

For good reason. Heather would have been incredibly upset.

"No. Not really. She's usually well behaved, but she does occasionally take off, so we can just be careful about keeping the door closed unless we're with her." She frowned down at the box. "What's in that, anyway?"

It looked like papers, and she suddenly realized it must have been the papers in her father's hutch drawer.

Chris cleared his throat. "Nothing. I mean, just some old work records your dad wanted me to sort through."

Heather's spine stiffened sharply as she realized what he'd said.

He'd just lied to her. Right to her face. She knew that wasn't what was in the boxes. It wasn't work related at all. Her father had told her what it was, and for some reason Chris didn't want her to know.

So he'd lied. He'd lied.

"Anyway," Chris said, turning away as if he once again wanted to change the subject, "I've got to go move my truck, since I left it at the curb. I'll be back."

She couldn't say anything in response. She couldn't speak at all. She was bombarded with wave after wave of confusion and fear and betrayal.

And she suddenly didn't care whether she was being reasonable or mature or emotionally healthy. Because she suddenly knew she'd been falling in love with a man who'd just stood there and lied to her.

She'd been trying to trust him, but she couldn't. She *couldn't.* Which meant there was no reason to assume he'd still be around ten years from now. Or even ten months from now.

She'd been so incredibly stupid to think that maybe he would.

She was so upset she was blinded by the emotion, and she would have cried if she hadn't been so frozen with the devastating revelation.

She had no idea what to do, what to say to him, what the best choice was for her to do right now.

All she knew was she had to get away.

The big decisions she'd have to save until later, but there was at least one small decision she could make right now.

"Come on, Lucy," she managed to choke, nuzzling the little dog for comfort. "We're not going to stay here

165

tonight. Not with someone who lies to us like that. Let's go spend the night at Dad's."

FOURTEEN

"What the hell are you doing?" Chris demanded. He'd been gone all of five minutes, only to come back and find Heather in her room, placing clothes in an overnight bag. She didn't answer him. Didn't even bother to look at him. "Is this because I left the door open and Lucy got out?" He cursed as he raked a hand through his hair. "I said I was sorry. It was stupid of me. It's not gonna happen again."

"I know," she said quietly.

He moved into her room, and kept moving, until he had Heather moving away from her luggage. "Then what's going on?"

"I need some time to think," she said slowly, carefully enunciating each word. "I... I just need a night away, that's all."

His eyes went wide. "All because Lucy got out? Don't you think that's a bit extreme?"

Heather rolled her eyes and went to move past him, but he wouldn't let her. "This isn't about Lucy," she said, suddenly snapping out of her composure and shoving his hands off her. "This is because I can't trust you!"

"So again I have to ask, why?" he asked, his voice growing louder with frustration. "What have I done that has you suddenly feeling like that?"

She huffed with frustration of her own. "You lied. You stood right there and lied to my face. Just like you lied about what you were talking to my dad about yesterday." She took a step back and began to pace. "I've never hid how I feel, Chris. You know that trust is a big thing for me. I don't like secrets, and I don't like being kept in the dark. But most of all, I hate being lied to!"

He stared hard at her for a solid minute. "Heather... I..."

She held up a hand to stop him. "I should have stuck with my initial instincts. I knew I couldn't trust you when you first came back. I knew it, and yet I let myself believe..." Her voice trailed off, thick with emotion.

He saw her eyes welling with tears, and it gutted him. "Can we please talk about this? You don't have to leave. This is your home too. Just give me a chance to explain."

She vehemently shook her head. "I told you I need a little space for the night. I gave you a chance. Multiple chances, and you chose to placate me rather than tell me the truth."

Chris had come to know her well enough to know that she was fighting with herself just as much as she was with him. The thing was, he couldn't keep doing this. Couldn't keep having this same argument with her—fighting with her, trying to prove himself and prove that he wasn't going to leave. It was exhausting. Which was exactly what he said to her.

"Oh, it's exhausting to you?" she mocked. "You think it's easy living with someone, sleeping with someone, who you can't trust?"

A low growl came out before he could stop it. "I *know* it's not because that's exactly how I feel!" he shouted, furious that she kept using that phrase to describe him. "I get it that you have issues—I really do. But I'm not your damn mother! I didn't walk out on you when you were a kid, and I'm tired of having to pay the price for what she did! If you need to deal with that situation, then call her up and get it off your chest, but quit taking it out on me!"

She gasped, her eyes going wide, but she stayed silent.

Now it was his turn to pace, almost tripping over Lucy. "I have tried to be patient, but you know what? You would make a saint crazy with your bullshit!"

Heather went to speak, but Chris immediately shot her down.

"No. You've had plenty to say about me, and I think it's only fair that I get to have my say." He paused and waited for her to argue, but she didn't. She sure as hell glared at him though. "I don't know what else I can possibly do to please you. It's impossible!"

"You can start by not lying…"

He glared at her. Hard. But more than anything, he was torn. He could easily sit here and tell her what she wanted to hear, but it wasn't his place, and to be honest, it pissed him off to no end that they were even having this discussion. Either she trusted him or she didn't.

And clearly, she didn't.

No matter what he did.

"You know what? You're not the only one with issues, Heather. You look at my leaving Preston three years ago like it was something I did to *you*. Did you ever bother to look at it from my point of view? Did you even think for just one minute of what I was going through and why I left?" He shook his head. "Of course not. That would mean depriving you of the chance to play the victim. Which you have made a fine art of."

"How dare you!" she cried.

"No, how dare *you*!" he snapped. "Not everything is about you! It wasn't three years ago, it wasn't yesterday or today, and it certainly wasn't when you were a kid and your mom left!" And then all the fight left him at the look of utter devastation on her face. He cursed under his breath. "You know what? Screw it. You want an out? You got it. I'm done. I guess you were right about one thing. I can't be trusted to stay. I'm outta here."

And then he stormed out, slamming the door behind him.

Chris stood there for a minute and tried to calm down, and he almost had, when he heard a small sound.

It was Lucy, crying on the other side of the door.

~

"Uh-oh…"

"Mind if I come in?" Chris asked.

Jace stepped aside and motioned for Chris to come in. "She was pissed about the dog, huh?"

For the next ten minutes, Chris reiterated everything that had happened while pacing back and forth in Jace's apartment.

"Okay, so I have to ask," Jace began. "Why did you leave three years ago?"

Chris shrugged and sat down on the sofa. "It was all too much. I'd lived here my whole life with my mother. She was the only family I had. And I sat here and had to watch her die. Every day for a year, I watched her get weaker and weaker—watched the cancer slowly eat away at her body. When she was gone… I was lost. I didn't know how to live here without her, while at the same time, it was too hard to stay here with all the memories."

Jace nodded sympathetically. "Damn, Chris. I'm sorry."

"I had always wanted to leave Preston. It's a great town, but I thought I wanted more. I stayed to help my mom. And then she got sick, and I knew I couldn't leave. After she died, I simply couldn't stay. I didn't even think about it. Didn't talk to anyone about it. I just packed up my shit and went in and saw Tom on my way out of town."

"Was he upset with you?"

Chris shook his head. "I think he was surprised—shocked really—but he understood. He never tried to stop me. If anything, he asked if I needed anything. Other than my mom, Tom's the closest person to a relative that I've ever had."

They sat in companionable silence for several minutes.

"It didn't take long for me to realize that I'd made a mistake. Preston was home. It just took a little prompting for me to come back."

"So what are you going to do?" Jace asked. "It seems to me that this situation with Heather isn't working out. You can't keep working together and living together while you're keeping a secret from her. And to be honest, it was kind of crappy of Tom to put you in that position. All those positions."

"I don't think—"

"No, here's the thing," Jace quickly interrupted. "You have to decide what it is that you want more—the business or Heather. Because this whole damn situation the way it is now isn't working for anyone. And if you want to know the truth from a guy who knows a thing or two about dysfunctional relationships, I can tell you that the business part of your relationship is going to just make things worse unless you can really figure this out."

"Shit," Chris murmured.

"Exactly. You've got work to do on both fronts, and it's going to be hard to do both at the same time. So which do you want more, the business or the relationship?"

That was the million-dollar question, wasn't it?

Jace got up, grabbed them both a beer and sat back down. Chris could see that he was trying to be respectful and not pressure Chris for an answer, but he also knew that he couldn't hide out here all night.

Putting his beer down on the coffee table, Chris pulled out his phone with a murmured, "Excuse me," to Jace and quickly pulled up Tom's number.

"Hey, Chris," Tom said cheerfully. "What's going on? A little late for a social call. Everything all right?"

"I can't do this anymore."

Tom was silent for a moment before saying, "You're going to have to be more specific. I'm not sure I know what exactly you're referring to."

"I want out of the business, Tom," Chris said, the words coming more easily than he imagined they would. "This whole situation… it's not working. Not for me, and especially not for Heather."

"I see."

"I don't think you really do," Chris interrupted. "I think your heart was in the right place, but somewhere along the line, things changed. Heather's upset and rightfully so. You asked me to lie to her, Tom. I've been trying so hard to get her to trust me, and we were finally on our way there, and then this whole situation came up."

"I didn't ask you to lie. If you lied to her, then you did that yourself. I get that you're mad at me, but don't be blaming me for a mess you made on your own. I'm sorry if I put you in an awkward position. I really am. But you know why I asked you not to mention this, Chris," Tom said. "And you said you understood."

"I do. I swear to you that I do, but Heather means more to me than anything else. I can find another job. Hell, I can find another place to live. But I can't find another Heather," he said gruffly. "She deserves the truth... from both of us. She's stronger than you think, and... she's hurting, Tom. Because of us." He cleared his throat. "Because of me."

"You know that's exactly what I was trying to keep from happening."

"I didn't betray your confidence. I want you to know that. But it cost me. I... I'm sorry, Tom, but you're going to have to come clean with your daughter because I'm not going to keep another secret from her. I love her. I want a life with her. But that's never going to happen if I'm torn in two directions."

"Chris," Tom began, suddenly sounding very weary, "I'm sorry it ended up tearing you up."

"And I don't mean to be blaming you for what happened. I've got stuff of my own I need to work on. I know that. But I just don't want to be put in this position again."

"So you won't be. We won't let it happen. You don't need to leave the company—"

"Yes. Yes, I do," Chris interrupted. "It's the only way for me to prove to Heather that she means the world to me. Let her have it, Tom. The business. The truth. She may be a grown woman, but she still needs her father."

"I know. But I wish you'd reconsider—"

"My decision's made. For the first time since I got back to Preston, I know I'm doing the right thing and for the right reason."

"I don't know what to say."

Chris smiled. "Say that you understand and you wish me luck."

"Always, son. Always."

When they hung up, Chris looked over at Jace and saw his friend smiling. "Well... I guess you heard."

Jace stood and picked up Chris's beer and handed it to him. "So what are you going to do? You know, for a job?"

"No idea," Chris said, but it didn't even bother him. He felt lighter and happier and... hopeful. "I'm not even going to worry about that right now. I've got some money saved up, and I know I'll be okay in that respect. Right now, I have to go and make sure that Heather's okay and work this out."

"You think she's going to be open to this? To you just walking away from the business? Isn't that feeding right into her crazy assumption about you?"

"She thinks I'm going to leave, and I'm not going to do that. I guess I'm going to find out if she was as serious about us being together as I was. For all I know, she may want us to stay as partners and quit seeing each other."

Jace's eyes went wide. "What are you going to do if she says that's what she wants? Will you go along with it?"

Chris opened his beer and took a long pull of it before putting the bottle back down on the coffee table. "Hell no. That's not even an option."

Jace grinned. "So?"

"So I'm going up there and putting it all on the line—it's her that I want, not her father's business. And I'll gladly go and flip burgers in town or go to work for another construction company—not as a foreman because I don't want to compete with her—if it means that we stay together."

"You're that serious about her?" Jace asked. "That sure?"

Chris nodded. "I've never been more sure about anything in my life."

"I envy you, man. I really do."

With a smile, Chris patted Jace on the back and turned to walk toward the door. "Don't envy me yet. This could all blow up in my face."

Jace laughed. "Nah. I don't think it's going to be easy, but you're not going to fail."

"From your lips to God's ears," Chris said with a wink as he walked out the door.

With his heart beating a little rapidly, he made his way back down to his apartment. But he stopped and did something he'd never done before first.

He knocked on Estelle's door.

"Who is it?" she snapped from the other side of the door. "What do you want? I have a gun!"

Chris chuckled. The woman was never boring, that was for sure. "Estelle? It's Chris. Can you open the door?"

She did and glared at him. "Of course I can open a door. You think I'm so old that I don't know how to open a door anymore?"

Rather than argue, he got right to the point. "I need to ask a favor, Estelle." Her eyes went wide, and she immediately began fussing with her curlers as if they were threatening to break free. "I need you to know that I'm going to go into my apartment and convince Heather that I love her."

"Oh… well…"

"It may get loud in there. We'll probably argue."

"That's not the way to convince a woman that you love her, Christopher. I thought you had better manners than that."

He smiled at her and laughed a little. "I do. But let's just say Heather and I have had a misunderstanding, and I'm hoping to throw myself at her feet and beg for mercy."

"Now that's more like it," Estelle beamed. "But what does this have to do with me?"

"I need to make sure that you're not going to come down the hall waving a golf club or a baseball bat at me. I wanted you to know what's going on so you don't have to be scared, and I wanted to tell you thank you."

One of her wrinkled hands fluttered over her heart. "Thank me? For what?"

"For always being concerned for us. I just didn't want to worry you tonight."

She blushed. "Christopher," she said softly, "that's one of the nicest things anyone's ever done for me."

He leaned in and kissed her on the cheek. "Now wish me luck!"

"Young man, you're not going to need it. Heather's far too crazy about you to let you get away!"

He grinned at her and winked. "Let's hope that you're right!" He waved and continued down the hall until he stopped at his door.

With a steadying breath, he let himself back in.

FIFTEEN

For ten minutes after Chris stormed out of the apartment, Heather could do nothing but sit in a stunned daze, occasionally petting Lucy when the dog came up and tried to nuzzle her.

Chris had left. For good. Just like she'd known he would eventually.

Maybe she'd overreacted earlier. Maybe she shouldn't have needed to get away from him for the night. But she hadn't known that was the end of the entire relationship.

Evidently, it was.

Chris always ran away. That was what he did.

She'd believed he was actually changing—just like she was—but maybe neither of them could really change.

She was too overwhelmed to even cry, although her throat was so tight she could barely breathe and her eyes had blurred over too much to see the details of the apartment. The beautifully updated kitchen. The old wooden floors. The big windows. Her favorite red chair. Flo.

The apartment would look strangely empty without that ugly old recliner.

She sucked in a hard breath, almost a sob, and reached for her phone, dialing the first person she thought of. It happened to be her dad.

"Hey, girl," he said warmly but rather hoarsely.

"I'm sorry. Were you asleep?"

"Nah. Just dozing. The game is boring. What's the matter?"

177

She had no idea how he'd known that something was wrong, when all she'd said were five normal words. "Nothing."

"Don't lie to your old dad. What's going on?"

The concern in his voice almost broke her. Her shoulders shook as she choked on a few silent sobs, trying to repress them so her father wouldn't hear.

He must have read into the silence though. "What made you cry, honey?"

The tears started falling then. "I think…" She took a ragged breath, trying to control her emotions enough to speak. "I think I blew things with Chris."

"Oh." He let out an audible sigh. "Shit."

"I blew it. I didn't trust him like I should have. And now he's taken off, and he's not going to come back."

"You don't know that for sure."

"He sounded pretty sure."

"Yeah, well, he might have thought so when he said it, but he really has changed, Heather. I don't think he'd walk out on you for good after just a fight."

"It was more than a fight."

"Maybe. Maybe not. Why did you think you couldn't trust him?"

Heather didn't usually tell her father the ins and outs of her romantic relationships, but she needed someone to talk to now, and her father was the person she trusted most. She sniffed and wiped away her tears, already feeling a little better from her dad's matter-of-fact common sense. "He was lying to me. I mean, I know there's something going on between you and him, but at least you didn't lie to me about it. He did. And it just… just triggered all my old insecurities."

"Insecurities are never as old as we want them to be."

"Exactly."

"I'm sorry we were keeping secrets from you, Heather. We thought… I thought it was for the best. The last thing I want to do is hurt you. But I guess I ended up hurting you more."

"It wasn't your fau—"

"Yeah, it was. I'm working on something. A new business idea. I wanted to get Chris's input on some stuff, but I was afraid it would bring up bad memories for you, so I asked him not to tell you until I knew for sure it was going to happen."

"What business idea?" Her head was spinning now as she tried to keep up with this new information.

"You know those birdhouses your mother and I used to build?"

The memory of it still stabbed. So many hours her parents had spent out in the backyard, working on those birdhouses while Heather played on the grass or climbed trees. "Yes," she whispered. "Of course."

"Well, I've been working on them again, and I thought I'd see if I could start selling them. It would be a good retirement project for me. I don't think I'm ready to sit around doing nothing yet."

She took three breaths in a row, fighting back her first instinct—which was that the birdhouses were tainted by her mother's memory. "If that's what you want to do, Dad, then of course I'll support you. You didn't have to hide it from me."

"I know the memories are hard for you, so I was just trying to be careful. I'm not sure if it will work out or not, so I didn't want to hurt you unnecessarily. But I can see now that I was wrong. I'm sorry, honey."

179

"It's okay. It really is. I know I overreacted and didn't treat Chris the way I should have. But the truth is…" She wiped away a few more tears. "The truth is, if he left because of this, then he would have left eventually anyway."

"That might be true—if he's actually left. I'm not sure that's the case."

"I wish I had your optimism."

"Not optimism. Experience. I've lived long enough to know love when I see it."

She gulped. "He doesn'—"

Her father laughed, interrupting her. "You don't have to believe me. But at least think about it and figure out what exactly you want."

"I know what I want." She wanted Chris. And, for the first time, she actually believed she was strong enough to be in a real relationship, to trust the way she should have all along.

"Then start thinking about how you can get it back."

She had no idea what to say to that, so she just mumbled, "Okay. Thanks, Dad."

"Anytime. Now, it really is my bedtime."

"Good night. I'll talk to you tomorrow."

She hung up the phone and looked down at Lucy, who was sitting at her feet, gazing up at her mournfully.

After a minute, Heather said, "You're right, Lucy. You're right. We belong here. I'm not going anywhere."

Lucy jumped up to her feet and panted.

"I shouldn't have tried to leave that way. It was wrong. And stupid. Chris is too good a guy to have lied to me like that without a good reason."

Lucy's tongue was hanging out now and she turned an excited circle.

"I don't know if he's going to come back," Heather continued, looking around the quiet apartment. There were signs of Chris all around. Not just Flo, but his shoes on the floor, his travel mug next to the sink, his laundry basket near his bedroom door, where he'd left it after doing laundry.

He belonged here. Exactly as she and Lucy did.

And she suddenly felt a swell of hope as she realized he might know it too. He'd been angry, but it might not have been his final decision. For once, she was going to really trust him.

"I know what I'm going to do," she told Lucy, who was doing a little happy dance, her claws tapping on the hardwood floor.

Heather started for the kitchen. "I'm going to make him cookies."

~

The cookies were almost done, filling the apartment with a warm, sweet fragrance, when Heather heard a sound at the door.

She whirled around, her heart coming alive when she saw Chris coming through the front door, looking tired and rumpled and determined.

He jerked to a stop when he saw her. "You're still here."

Her heart sank. "You thought I'd be gone?"

"I didn't know. Weren't you going to leave?"

"I was before. But not now. So you aren't here to see me?"

He shook his head, as if trying to shake himself back to focus. "I was hoping you weren't gone, but I didn't know for sure."

"I'm still here." She gave him a wobbly smile. "I thought *you* might be gone."

He strode over to her, his expression changing in a way that took her breath away. "I should never have walked out. I even tried to blame your dad for it, when it was always my own fault. I was just doing what I always do, but I don't want to be that person anymore. I'm here, Heather." He took both her hands in his. "And I'm staying."

She swallowed hard, realizing that her hope in him had been fully justified, more than justified. There was no denying that look in his eyes. He wasn't going anywhere. "For good?"

"For good. Please tell me that's what you want too. I love you, Heather. I know I might not have always acted like it, but I do. There's never been anyone but you for me, and that's never going to change. It's okay if you're not there yet. I can wait. I just want you to know that I know what I want now, and I'm willing to do whatever it takes to get it. To get *you*."

She swayed on her feet. She'd been hoping for maybe an admission of feelings, but she'd never expected this. "Really?" she asked stupidly.

He gave a little huff of amusement. "Really. I want to be your roommate for a really long time."

The dry irony in his voice actually helped her pull herself together. She slanted him a teasing little look. "I want to be your roommate too—as long as that comes with certain benefits we can negotiate later and as long as you can put up with Lucy."

Lucy had been snuffling around Chris's feet since he'd entered. He leaned over to give the dog a little pet. "I'm happy to put up with Lucy, as long as you can put up with Flo."

She laughed out loud, almost hugging herself with excitement. It was like a miracle—like the worst night had suddenly transformed into the best. "That sounds like a fair deal. I talked to my dad. I know about his business, and why you lied to me. I still wish you hadn't, but I understand. I'm sorry I blew up the way I did."

"No. I get it. I shouldn't have lied, no matter what your dad asked me to do. If I'm in this relationship, then I need to be in it all the way. No lies or secrets. And I called your dad too and told him that if it's going to hurt you, then I don't want to be a partner in the business at all."

She gasped. "No!"

"No, what?"

"No, you can't pull out! I need you! The business needs you. I want to be your partner and your roommate and... and everything."

His face relaxed in a smile, and she knew in that instant that he'd just gotten everything he wanted.

And apparently, what he wanted most of all was her.

Chris sniffed the air. "What's that smell?"

Heather gasped. "My cookies!" She ran over to pull out the sheet from the oven, relieved when she saw that they were a little more done than she preferred but not at all burned.

"Why were you making cookies?" Chris asked, coming to look over her shoulder with interest.

"I was making them for you."

Chris stiffened. "You were?"

"Yeah," she admitted, lowering her gaze. "I was hoping you were coming back, so I wanted… I wanted to do something nice for you."

Chris made a rough sound in his throat and he pulled her into his arms.

The cookies were completely forgotten for the next half hour.

~

A week later, Heather woke up when it was still dark in the room. Glancing over, she saw it wasn't even five o'clock.

She started to roll over and go back to sleep for another hour, but as she turned over she bumped into something big and warm and hard.

Chris. He must have crept over onto her side of the bed as they slept.

Typical. The man just filled up every space he stepped into.

She gave the covers a hard tug and then tried to push him over to his side, but he didn't budge. He was sound asleep, and his body just wouldn't move.

She gave him another push, and this time he huffed and woke up.

"Whuz goin' on?" he mumbled.

"You're on my side of the bed."

"What's wrong with that?" He sounded a lot more awake now.

"I don't have any room!"

"Why do you need room?"

"Everyone needs room to sleep. You think I can sleep on three inches of the bed?"

"I think there's nothing wrong with sleeping right next to me." His voice had changed now. It sounded like he was smiling, and he reached out to pull her against him.

She'd been serious about getting another hour of sleep, but now that she was hearing his voice, so thick and fond and sleepy, she decided it wasn't the worst idea in the world to get a little closer to him. "I thought guys were the ones who liked to have their space."

"We do. Unless sex is involved. Then we don't need any space at all." He rolled her on top of him and slid his hands down to cup her bottom.

"And you think sex is somehow involved right now."

She could feel that it was, in fact, involved. He was starting to get hard beneath her.

"I think you know the answer to that," he drawled.

She couldn't help but smile as she found his face in the dark and kissed him.

They kept kissing as Chris stroked over her body, teasing and fondling all the intimate parts of her until she was just as turned on as he was. Then they fumbled with each other's clothes until they were both naked.

Both of them were smiling as he slid himself inside her and she wrapped her legs around him.

"I think," she murmured, adjusting herself around his hard length, "if more roommates had mornings like this, people would be falling all over themselves to find a roommate."

He chuckled, his whole body shuddering deliciously from the amusement. "Well, no one else can have my roommate. She's already claimed."

She sucked in a sharp breath as he started to move. "So is mine. So is mine."

They moved together in a practiced rhythm, the bed shaking and both of them starting to pant loudly as their motion became more and more urgent. Chris kissed her occasionally, and he managed to hold out until her body tightened down in an orgasm. As she was crying out her pleasure, he let go, so both of them were coming down together, breathless and satisfied.

They were still smiling as they relaxed, and Chris rolled over onto his back and nestled her against him.

"And we still have a while to doze until it's time to get up," Heather murmured happily.

"It's a very good morning." Chris stroked her hair, his body hot and relaxed.

They were starting to drift off when there was a sudden hop on the bed. Lucy ran up to nuzzle first Chris and then Heather.

Chris groaned. "What does she want?"

"She thinks it's time to go out. We must have woken her up."

Chris groaned again.

Heather didn't want to move, but Lucy was her dog, and the poor thing wasn't going to stop nagging until she'd gotten outside. Heather started to sit up. "I'll take her."

"Nah," Chris said, heaving himself out of bed before Heather could get into a sitting position. "I'll do it." He snagged a pair of sweats from the floor and pulled them on. "Come on, girl."

"Thank you," Heather called, filled with such affection she was momentarily choked up. He was in her life to stay. She knew it. He was going to be there for her today and tomorrow and the next day. She no longer had any doubts. "I love you! You're the best roommate in the world."

Chris chuckled as he and Lucy left the bedroom. "Right back at you."

EPILOGUE

Three months later

"So... this."

Chris nodded. "Yup. This."

Jace Foster shook his head sadly as he looked down. "I never thought... I don't know. I guess I'm just a little stunned."

"It's not the end of the world. If I can handle it, so can you."

Looking up, Jace gave him a look of disbelief. "Are you sure? Are you sure you're handling it? Because this seems like you're going a little off the deep end."

Smiling, Chris gave his friend a pat on the back. "And someday, you'll know exactly how it feels."

"God, I hope not," Jace murmured. "Not like this. I'm already in my own form of hell."

"Dude, you're going to have to do something about that. Take the risk. What have you got to lose?"

"Um, everything?" he said with a nervous laugh. "You don't think I've pondered this a million times?"

"And yet here you are."

"It's not the same. You and Heather... it was different."

"You can't keep ignoring the situation. Maybe it's time for you and Isabella to—"

"To what?" Jace quickly interrupted. "To stop being friends? Because that's what's going to happen if I tell her how I feel. Don't you think if she was interested in me, I would know?"

"I had no idea that Heather had ever been into me."

"That was different. The two of you weren't that close before you left. You were older. Hung out with a different crowd of people. It wasn't like you saw each other every day." He stopped and sighed. "I may not be the most observant guy on the planet, but I'm pretty sure I would have noticed if Isabella's feelings had changed—if she thought of me as anything more than a friend."

Chris studied him for a minute. "I saw her out the other night with Mike Taney."

Jace's hands clenched into fists at his side as he glared at Chris.

"Seems like a nice guy. They were walking along the boardwalk, laughing." He took a moment to gage Jace's reaction, and it was just as he expected—his friend was not happy with the thought of Isabella out with Mike. Or any guy. "Mike's a lawyer now, from what I understand. Makes good money. Hard to believe he's still single."

Jace sighed loudly. "Just what exactly are you getting at?"

"Just stating some facts."

"Oh yeah? Well, your facts suck."

That had Chris laughing. "Well, you better get used to them, because if you don't do something—and soon—you're going to have to get used to good ol' Mike hanging around. Or some other guy. Someone who's not afraid to let her know how they feel. And how are you going to handle that?"

"I... I don't know. Maybe if I could..."

Chris put his hand on Jace's shoulder. "Just think about it, okay? Take it from someone who's been there."

They both turned at the sound of a door slamming out in the parking lot. Standing in the lobby getting their mail had gone from a quick hello to a deep conversation. Chris saw Heather walking their way and sighed.

"Again, you sure?" Jace asked.

Heather walked through the door carrying a couple of grocery bags and one of her father's birdhouses. She smiled at them both.

"Absolutely," Chris said softly.

"Hey, you two," Heather said when she got closer and leaned in to give Chris a proper kiss hello. Then she bent down to give Lucy a pat on the head. "Has she gone out already, or were you heading out?"

"We were on our way in when I ran into Jace." Taking the bags from her hands, Chris waved to his neighbor and then led Heather down the hall and up the stairs to their apartment. Once inside, they worked together to get Lucy off the leash and to put the groceries away.

"So another birdhouse, huh?"

Her soft chuckle was her immediate response. "I can't help it. This one reminded me of a cabin we rented when I was a little girl. My parents used to book the same one up in the mountains every year, and we used to have a great time there." She paused. Smiled. Then shrugged. "It was always a great memory, so when I saw Dad had made this one, I just had to have it."

With a quick kiss on her forehead, Chris turned back to finish putting the last of the food away.

"I know we talked about grilling tonight, but I'm not sure I'm up for it. It was a mentally exhausting day. So much paperwork to go through now that we're getting ready to meet with the lawyers for Dad to sign over the business. I had no idea there would be so much. By the time I left, I swear my eyes were starting to cross!"

He chuckled and then reached over to the table and picked up a large envelope. "Then maybe you should wait to see this until tomorrow," he said, hesitantly handing the large envelope over to her.

She groaned softly and noticed the label had their company logo on it. "What's this?"

Shrugging, Chris went over to the pantry to get Lucy's food. "No idea. It's addressed to you."

"I can see that," she said, more to herself than him. "But why would anyone in the office mail something to me when I'm there all day? And I handle most of the mail."

"I guess you'll just have to read it to find out," he said lightly. Moving around her, he put food in Lucy's bowl and almost willed the dog to scarf it down faster than she usually did while Heather scanned the papers she'd pulled from the envelope.

"What the... I don't..." She flipped the first page over and her expression went from confusion, to disbelief, to a full blown smile. And when she turned around, she found Chris on one knee. She gasped—her hands covering her mouth for a brief moment. The papers fell softly to the floor. "What are you..."

Chris was on one knee, holding Lucy in one hand against his chest. "Heather Carver, I love you."

Her eyes welled with tears as she smiled and nodded at him. "I love you too."

"I have loved being your roommate, and I love being partners in business with you. But next week marks the end of our original arrangement, and I'd like to... propose something to you."

The look of confusion was back on her face, and he loved it. Loved the little wrinkle in her forehead and the way her lips pursed just a little bit.

"So you've glanced at my contract," he began and then nodded toward the papers she'd dropped on the table when she spotted him on one knee. "You should probably refer to that now."

Without questioning him, Heather picked up the papers and straightened them quickly before looking at him.

"Article one," he said, his voice strong and confident. "We extend our lease here in Preston's Mill with one minor change."

Heather glanced at the paper and smiled. "We make one of the bedrooms an office and move into the other—together."

Chris nodded firmly. "All those in agreement, raise your hand."

And they both did.

"Excellent. Article two. Food."

Laughing softly, Heather glanced at the paper and then back to him with one arched brow. "Seriously?"

He nodded. "Joint food shopping. One budget for the two of us. Takeout twice a week, dinner out once a week and you bake cookies at least once a week. Preferably twice."

"Chris…"

"All those in agreement, raise your hand." He quickly raised his and then watched her until she reluctantly raised her hand.

"Very good." He cleared his throat. "Article three." He paused and thought for a moment, trying to remember which one came next.

"Laundry," Heather provided.

"That's right. Laundry. I'm thinking…"

"You can scratch that last paragraph off the list," she quickly interrupted, even as she laughed. "I don't consider Naked Saturday a way to cut back on water and laundry. Just… no."

Shaking his head, Chris looked at Lucy. "I tried." Then he looked at Heather and winked. "Fine. Laundry rules stay as they always were. We can initial the change."

Heather nodded. "Good to know." Then she flipped the page and frowned. "It says article four, but then there isn't anything there."

"Lucy wanted to present that one herself."

The bland look Heather gave him showed that she thought he was crazy. "Really. Lucy's going to present article four."

He nodded. "It's really not nice to publicly shame her like that you know," he admonished. "Can she help it that she has limited verbal skills that normally only extend to letting us know when she's hungry and has to poop?"

"Is that what article four is about? Better communications?"

Looking at Lucy sympathetically, Chris whispered in the dog's ear, "You're going to really have to pull this off without a hitch. I had no idea your mistress had such doubts about how smart you are."

"I didn't say I had doubts," Heather laughed.

Chris put Lucy down and nudged her toward Heather. "Go ahead, girlie. Show her what you've got."

Crouching down, Heather watched as her little dog pranced over to her. "Hey, sweet girl. You have something to say to me?"

Lucy barked and danced around Heather's ankles.

Chris waited until she was back in front of Heather before telling her to sit—which she immediately obeyed.

"Good one," Heather cooed. "But sitting has never been the problem."

"Give her a minute," Chris commented. "Lucy, give Heather your paw."

And with a happy little yip, Lucy held up her paw.

"Aww, good girl!" Heather said with a smile and shook the little dog's paw.

"I bought her a new collar," Chris said. "But you may want to check it out and make sure it's okay for her."

Leaning forward, Heather took a closer look and then gasped. "Chris," she said reverently as she reached out for Lucy. "What did you do?"

He came closer, laid down on his stomach next to the dog and fiddled with her collar until the sparkling charm he'd put there came off. Then he held it out to Heather. "She insisted on wearing it, but I warned her that she'd be the envy of the neighborhood if she wore this much bling."

Lucy barked her disagreement, and they both laughed.

"Heather Carver, I love you. You're more to me than a roommate and business partner. You're my life. And I want to spend the rest of my life with you—being your friend, your lover, your roommate, your partner, and your husband. Will you marry me?"

Wordlessly, she nodded and then gasped with delight as he slid the ring on her finger—much to Lucy's distress.

Back up on his knees, Chris drew Heather to him and kissed her—thoroughly, deeply and with everything he had. When they finally broke apart, Lucy was still barking and with an exaggerated eye roll, Chris reached into his pocket and pulled out a different ring. It had a pink bedazzled charm that read "Lucy." Carefully, he placed it back on her collar and then picked her up and kissed her on the head. Heather did the same.

"Oh, you're good," Heather said, still smiling.

"Have to take care of my girls. I can't be showing favorites."

"Hey!" She was trying to sound indignant, but she ended up laughing. "You're amazing. Really. It means a lot to me that you love us both."

Reaching down, Chris placed his hands over Lucy's ears and then whispered, "I love you a whole lot more."

Then Heather removed his hands from the dog and lifted them to her body and said, "She'll have to get used to sharing you, then."

And he readily agreed.

ABOUT NOELLE ADAMS

Noelle handwrote her first romance novel in a spiral-bound notebook when she was twelve, and she hasn't stopped writing since. She has lived in eight different states and currently resides in Virginia, where she writes full time, reads any book she can get her hands on, and offers tribute to a very spoiled cocker spaniel.

She loves travel, art, history, and ice cream. After spending far too many years of her life in graduate school, she has decided to reorient her priorities and focus on writing contemporary romances. For more information, please check out her website: noelle-adams.com.

Books by Noelle Adams

Tea for Two Series
>Falling for her Brother's Best Friend
>Winning her Brother's Best Friend
>Seducing her Brother's Best Friend

Balm in Gilead Series
>Relinquish
>Surrender
>Retreat

Rothman Royals Series
>A Princess Next Door
>A Princess for a Bride
>A Princess in Waiting
>Christmas with a Prince

Preston's Mill Series (co-written with Samantha Chase)
    Roommating
    Speed Dating
    Procreating

Eden Manor Series
    One Week with her Rival
    One Week with her (Ex) Stepbrother
    One Week with her Husband
    Christmas at Eden Manor

Beaufort Brides Series
    Hired Bride
    Substitute Bride
    Accidental Bride

Heirs of Damon Series
    Seducing the Enemy
    Playing the Playboy
    Engaging the Boss
    Stripping the Billionaire

Willow Park Series
    Married for Christmas
    A Baby for Easter
    A Family for Christmas
    Reconciled for Easter
    Home for Christmas

One Night Novellas
    One Night with her Best Friend

One Night in the Ice Storm
One Night with her Bodyguard
One Night with her Boss
One Night with her Roommate
One Night with the Best Man

The Protectors Series (co-written with Samantha Chase)
Duty Bound
Honor Bound
Forever Bound
Home Bound

Standalones
A Negotiated Marriage
Listed
Bittersweet
Missing
Revival
Holiday Heat
Salvation
Excavated
Overexposed
Road Tripping
Chasing Jane
Late Fall
Fooling Around
Married by Contract
Trophy Wife
Bay Song

ABOUT SAMANTHA CHASE

New York Times and USA Today Bestseller/contemporary romance writer Samantha Chase released her debut novel, Jordan's Return, in November 2011. Although she waited until she was in her 40's to publish for the first time, writing has been a lifelong passion. Her motivation to take that step was her students: teaching creative writing to elementary age students all the way up through high school and encouraging those students to follow their writing dreams gave Samantha the confidence to take that step as well.

When she's not working on a new story, she spends her time reading contemporary romances, blogging, playing way too many games of Scrabble on Facebook and spending time with her husband of 25 years and their two sons in North Carolina. For more information visit her website at www.chasing-romance.com.

Books by Samantha Chase

Jordan's Return
The Christmas Cottage
Ever After
Catering to the CEO
In the Eye of the Storm
Wait for Me
Trust in Me
Stay With Me
A Touch of Heaven
Mistletoe Between Friends
The Snowflake Inn
The Baby Arrangement
Baby, I'm Yours

Baby, Be Mine
Exclusive
Moonlight in Winter Park
Duty Bound
Honor Bound
Forever Bound
Home Bound
The Wedding Season
Return to You
Meant for You
I'll Be There
Made for Us
Live, Love & Babies Trilogy
Love Walks In
Christmas in Silver Bell Falls
Waiting for Midnight
Always My Girl

Website: www.chasing-romance.com
Facebook: www.facebook.com/SamanthaChaseFanClub
Twitter: https://twitter.com/SamanthaChase3
Pinterest: http://www.pinterest.com/samanthachase31/

64868695R00124

Made in the USA
Columbia, SC
12 July 2019